The Magician Who Sold God

A Fictional Novel by

Ambrose T. Mpofu

Goldring Publishing

New Zealand

The book is dedicated to my two daughters Thoko and

Sindy. The story is written in remembrance of my late

mother whom I still miss so much.

Chapter 1: Growing up in the township

Angelbert Ncube was born in October 1976 to a small family of three children, two boys, Themba and Don, and a girl, Sihle. When Angel was born, Themba had just started school and was seven years old. Sihle was five years old and about to start school, while Don was three years old.

Angelbert's family was considered relatively small in the dusty Bulawayo townships in the seventies. Other families in Angelbert's neighbourhood had eight children with some big families having up to ten. One of Angelbert's neighbours had four wives and twenty-two children. In most cases, the bigger the family, the poorer they seemed to be and the less educated the parents were. This was not always true; as in the case of a family who lived three houses from where the Ncubes lived, they were a large family that was apparently well off by township standards even though the parents had never been to school. In Angelbert's neighbourhood, the houses were three-roomed and were composed of a kitchen, lounge and a bedroom. Most families built extra rooms outside the main house which were either used as extra bedrooms or were rented out to supplement the family's income. Angel's parents could not afford to build the extra outside

rooms, so their kitchen doubled up as the boys'
bedroom.

Simon, Angelbert's father, worked at a local garment
factory in Bulawayo's industrial area. His mother, Siza,
was a full-time house wife, who generated extra income
by selling vegetables outside the beer hall every night.
Simon's wages were just enough for the family to
survive from hand to mouth. He cycled to and from
work and when the bicycle was broken down he walked
for an hour and half to work. Hundreds of other
workers either walked or cycled to work too. The
majority of unskilled industrial workers were very lowly
paid; their wages were more like wedges. Instead of
being the amount of money paid per week for services
by an employee, they were more like a piece of wood
employees were given to wedge themselves and their
families from falling into starvation. The wages were
just enough for them to stay alive and come back to
work.

In order to provide a decent life for their big
families, it was very common to find families with
second homes in the rural areas where they did
subsistence farming. They kept a small farming plot,
cattle, goats, sheep and chickens. These animals were
the real wealth of the family. In this kind of set-up, the
wife would live in the rural home and the father and

school-going children lived in the township during the school days. The children would then join their mother during school holidays, with the father going to the rural home once a month, usually after pay day.

Simon and his family did not have this option. Simon was born in Malawi and came to the then Rhodesia when he was seven years old. Simon's parents came to Rhodesia during the 1950s when the British colonial rulers were encouraging the formation of the Federation of Rhodesia and Nyasaland. The federation was being created to counter the introduction of apartheid in South Africa and as a small appeasement to black nationalists in Nyasaland (later called Malawi), Northern Rhodesia (later called Zambia) and Southern Rhodesia (later called Rhodesia then Zimbabwe) who were calling for independence. Citizens from these three countries were free so travel throughout the region and seek employment.

Simon's parents put him through primary education but could not afford to send him for secondary education. Secondary school was considered highly educated for black people and Simon's father, who worked as a labourer for the then Rhodesia Railways, considered it unnecessary and regarded Simon as educated enough at primary school level, even though he had come out at the bottom of the class. His father adopted the Ncube surname when he registered Simon into school for the first time, rather than use his original Malawian surname of Lungu, to spare his son from the xenophobia of the local black Rhodesian. This did not completely stop the discrimination, but it made it happened less often. The three-roomed municipal rented house in which Simon was raising his family was inherited from his parents when they died as he was the only male child in the family even though he was the last born child. He had two sisters who arrived in Rhodesia ages ten and thirteen.

Angelbert was named so after his parents and family friends considered events immediately after his birth nothing short of a miracle.

At the time of his birth, doctors declared him stillborn. Immediately after he was born, he was washed and dressed in the clothes that his parents had brought to the hospital. He was then given to his mother, aunts and grandmothers to hold. He was kept with the family for the rest of that morning for about three hours. When the family was preparing to go home around midday and the hospital was making arrangements to take him to the crematorium, everyone, including the doctors and nurses, was bewildered and pleasantly surprised when he started to cry. There was so much joy, confusion and shock in the hospital ward at the unfolding events. He was called a miracle baby and his parents later abandoned the original name, John, that they had prepared to give him, and decided to call him their angel and gave him the name Angelbert, meaning a bright Angel.

Living in the dusty townships of Bulawayo was a daily struggle. For the Ncube children, there was never enough to eat. Like most children in the township, they went to school having had a breakfast that consisted of one slice of bread with nothing on it and a cup of black, sugarless tea. On a good day, they would also have a bowl of porridge before leaving for school. The next meal would usually be after school and would generally consist of the same as in the morning. School ended after midday, before sports training which was usually from 2pm to 5pm. The biggest meal of the day was the late evening dinner, in which of the four to five days of the week would be isitshwala, sadza or pap, a thickened porridge made from white meal-mealie and sour milk or dried green vegetables known locally as mufushwa. If they were lucky they would have sadza with fresh vegetables from their small garden. Angel, as he was called by his family and friends, despised the dried vegetables because sometimes he found sand when eating it. This was because they were dried in a dusty open space and sometimes dust settled on the drying leaves. He considered it the perfect example of poverty, any lower than this, they would be eating sand.

The three boys in the Ncube household all ate together from one bowl of pap and another bowl of milk, Sihle ate with her mother. Whoever ate the quickest or scooped the largest size of pap usually would go fulfilled more than the slow eaters. It was survival of the quickest. Angel, being the youngest, got used to going to bed hungry. Everyone called him Angel except his mother who preferred to call him Angie. He never liked this nickname as other kids on the street said it sounded like a girl's name. This did not stop his mother from calling him Angie at least until he had his first child. Simon, as the bread winner, got to eat from his own special plates. He got the best of every meal, or sometimes had his meals cooked separately. If there was any meat, only Simon ate it. The closest the children got to eating meat was having pap with the meat soup.

The celebration of birthdays, including presents and children's parties, was never heard of in the Ncube household. It was a luxury Simon and many other parents could not afford. For a family of twelve they would have had to celebrate an average of one party a month. Children's birthdays came and went without even a mention of the word and some children never even knew their own birthdays, later on know their siblings'. Angel, his brothers and sister and all their friends dreamt about getting out of the township as successful individuals and doing better than their parents, but it was all a game of chances. The odds were worse if one did not get good grades at school. There were some success stories though. Angel's neighborhood produced some very successful international musicians, footballers and businessmen. Of Angel's generation, an estimated one out of twenty children succeeded in creating a better life for themselves and became productive citizens. This included Angel himself, although for him it would turn out to be luck rather than design.

For some children in the township, luck was not on their side. One small petty criminal mistake completely changed their lives forever. One small wrong turn that would otherwise be considered silly mischief in other circumstances, in the township it would change your life forever.

Two of Don's school mates epitomised what could go wrong for teenagers in the township. During their second year at secondary school, they decided they did not like the way their mathematics teacher was treating them. He was one of the most dedicated teachers who wanted to see all his students do well. He conducted mathematics tests every Friday, and those who did not do well would be detained after class for extra lessons.

These two students were detained almost every Friday. Friday after school was the time all students looked forward to, particularly if there were sports competitions where their school would be competing against other schools either in athletics, soccer or netball. These were the only sports opportunities available to township schools. These two boys, although not gifted academically, were very good soccer players and the school team did very well when they were playing. They were also playing for the local premier club's junior team and had promising football careers ahead of them. As a result, they resented the Friday detentions, particularly if it meant they missed their soccer game. As part of the school policy, good grades came first and sports came second. If a teacher deemed students were not performing well in class, they had the right to pull them off the sports team even if they were the team's best player.

Unfortunately, this teacher was a heavy drinker and most students knew which beer hall him and other teachers frequented. They needed to have this information in order to know which places to avoid. So one Saturday night, the two students decided to wait for their mathematics teachers outside the beer hall and confront him about their Friday detentions. They were hoping that if they put pressure on him outside the school, he would ease up on their detentions. In his drunken state, the teacher was in no mood to entertain their demands. He just told them off and said they should be grateful that he was sacrificing his own unpaid time for their benefit. This did not go down well with the two boys and they decided to assault him. The fist fight ended tragically with the teacher, in his drunken state, losing his balance and falling, hitting his head on the concrete pavement edge. He was knocked unconscious and was later taken to hospital. Being in the township, the ambulance took several hours to arrive. By the time it turned up the teacher was soaking wet. This was because someone in the quickly gathered crowd had poured cold water on him thinking he had fainted or was too drunk and the cold water would help him to sober up quickly. He never regained consciousness and was in a coma for three weeks before doctors and his family decided he was so brain dead he would never regain consciousness, and turned off his life support machine.

Immediately after the incident, the two boys were expelled from school and arrested. They were charged with assault. Three weeks after their arrest and while in custody waiting for trial, their charges turned from common assault to murder. Without the benefit of their own lawyers, they were represented in their court cases by underpaid and overworked public defenders. Their public defenders did not even take a close look at the evidence or investigate the real cause of death. They assumed they were just another lot of township thugs who had no regard for the law and were most likely guilty.

Had all the evidence been examined, the courts would have found that the teacher's fall had nothing to do with the blows he received during the assault. The two boys' physical builds were so small compared to their teacher that it was next to impossible for them to hit him so hard that he would fall and hit his head on the pavement. It was not even mentioned during the court proceedings that the teacher was an alcoholic and was drunk on the night of the fight. Had he fallen because of his drunken state or tripped, he most likely would have suffered the same fate. The boys were just at the wrong place at the wrong time, they just precipitated an accident that was waiting to happen.

In a desire to see the case over quickly without any interest in justice, their public defenders did not bother to prepare for their defense, but just advised them to plead guilty so they would receive a lenient sentence. A stupid mistake, a bad justice system and the accident of being born in the township came together to condemn the two boys for a murder they did not commit.

After their conviction, their lives went from bad to worse. Tried as juveniles, they were sentenced to juvenile detention for five years each. Since they were both fifteen, this meant that two of their last years in detention would be spent at an adult detention facility.

Detention centres, whether juvenile or adult, where considered criminal universities. Almost all the township youths and adults who went to jail came back as hardened criminals with a much higher chance of going back to prison for other crimes than those who had never been in prison.

In the townships, opportunities to succeed in life were remote if one did not have a criminal record; for those with criminal records, it was virtually impossible to make an honest, successful living. So most convicts resorted to what they knew best, criminal activity. This was the case with these two boys and this was the life in the township. Fortunately, none of Simon's children got involved in petty criminal activity during their school days. Their mother was a strict no-nonsense lady.

Angel started primary school after he turned six years old. Life was not only tough at home, but school was no better either. He was not one of the brightest kids in class. Sitting in class with a growling stomach on a daily basis distracted his concentration to what the teacher was saying, making his ability to learn worse.

The school teachers were not very sympathetic; they had very little tolerance for poor performers like him. They had thirty-four other pupils to look after. Failing to answer questions or class tests always resulted in a caning, usually with a very hard stick on his hands. None of his brothers or sisters were doing well enough at school to be able to help him when he got home. He got used to being a subject of ridicule in class as he never raised his hand to answer any questions or actively took part in class. If the teacher picked him to answer a question, there was always a ninety-nine percent chance he would get it wrong. The best times of the day for him were play time and going home time.

The year Angel started second grade seemed to be going very well. He was placed in a class with one of the best teachers. She had the best pass rate of any second grade township school in Bulawayo. She was known to dedicate her own unpaid time, including weekends, to teach underperforming students. She even visited their parents to get them to work with her, if she thought that would help students perform better. She was the only teacher who did not believe in physically punishing failing students and was known to have never caned anyone for failing a test. Both students and parents respected and admired her. School was a bit more enjoyable for Angel; he felt confident enough to actively take part in class activities.

July of that year changed everything for the Ncube family.

On a Friday night, 16 July, their father, Simon, did not make it home at his usual time. Instead, around 8pm, two policemen came to their house to tell them that Simon had been involved in a road accident and had died at the scene. On his way home from work, he had been cycling along his usual route, which passed by the gates of a previously whites-only boys high school. Although black students were now allowed to register at the school, ninety-five percent of the students were whites. A car driven by one of the students had come from inside the school and failed to give way at the school gate, hitting Simon and two other cyclists. Simon had died at the scene and the other two cyclists were seriously injured.

It turned out that the students at the school were celebrating winning the national rugby championship they had won that day. This particular group of four white boarding school students got into a car belonging to one of the senior students who was himself not in the car when the accident happened. He had, however, given permission for the driver to take his car to go and buy more alcohol even though he knew that the student did not have a driver's license. The four students were all drunk. They decided to take the short drive to the nearest liquor outlet before it closed for the day. A long convoy of cyclists was coming from the nearby industrial area and was passing by the school gates. They did this every weekday, morning and evening, and on Saturday mornings and afternoons. Due to impaired judgment and lack of driving skills, the driver sped out of the school gates and ploughed through the three cyclists, including Simon, killing him instantly. What angered the other black cyclist was that all four students, visibly drunk and still carrying beer bottles, were more concerned about the damage to the car than the dead and injured black men.

The school authorities, all white males, were at the scene in a matter of minutes. They ordered all the students back into the school and locked the gates without bothering to call an ambulance or the police. They also took the car, which was still drivable but had a broken windscreen and other superficial damages, with them. Other cyclists went to the nearby shops and called the police and an ambulance. It was only two years after independence and life for black people had not changed much. Some white people's attitudes towards blacks had not changed either.

Life seemed to take a turn for the worse for Angel and his siblings. They had now lost their main bread winner. It would be impossible to survive on their mother's small earnings from selling vegetables. At six years old, Angel could not fully comprehend what was going on. He asked Themba why his mother was crying so much and why all these people had gathered at their house. He wanted to know why they all seemed sad and were crying all the time. Themba told him that his father was dead and would never be coming home again. To him, it felt like his father had just gone somewhere for some time and would be coming back one day.

The mourning went on for seven days until Simon was buried exactly a week and a day after the accident. All the mourners then dispersed at the end of that weekend and the Ncubes were left alone to continue their life without Simon. Their mother decided to move Sihle from sleeping in the sitting-cum-dining room to sleep with her in the bedroom. She moved the boys to the sitting room. The sitting-cum-dining room was also going to be used for cooking meals. She then rented out the kitchen in order to supplement the family's income.

The Ncubes got three thousand dollars from Simon's employer. He had worked for the company for eighteen years. Their mother had never had so much money at once in her entire life, and it seemed like a lot of money at the time. For a while, the family was going to survive comfortably, but it looked like the future would be bleak once the money ran out.

Police charged the teenage driver who killed Simon with culpable homicide, driving without a license and driving under the influence. So soon after independence, the killing of a black person by a white person was not considered a serious crime by a slowly reforming but still institutionally racist system. In this case, the police were white, the lawyer and state prosecutors were white and the judge was white. The only black people involved in this case were Simon and the two injured cyclists, none of whom were independently represented in any of the court proceedings.

The driver pleaded guilty to the culpable homicide charge and was fined for driving without a license. The charge of driving under the influence could not be proven because the police did not test the driver for alcohol in his system, either by breath testing or blood testing, on the day of the accident. The judge sentenced him to a one year suspended sentence on condition that he compensated Simon's family and the two injured cyclists and not commit similar offences in the next five years. The compensation figures were to be negotiated between the defendant and the three parties. If no agreement could be reached, the judge would then make the final determination. Simon's family was given two thousand dollars as compensation, while the injured cyclists were given five hundred dollars each.

To the injured parties, this seemed like a lot of money considering their monthly wages were a hundred dollars a month. Since they had not been represented in court they had no knowledge that the compensation amounts were supposed to be negotiated. The defendant's lawyers handed them the cash compensations and got them to sign a statement with fine print that stated they had negotiated and agreed to the amounts. All three people who signed on behalf of the families could not read or write later or understand the legal language. This outcome was a good outcome compared to a similar case before. Other criminal cases that involved a white person killing a black person resulted in the victim being blamed and the perpetrator acquitted by the courts, if the case was lucky enough to ever make it to the courts.

It was tradition for most primary schools in the townships to hire entertainers at the end of each school term. These included clowns, acrobats and magicians among others. Children were asked to pay a small fee to see the entertainment. Part of the money was used to pay the performers and some of it went to other school programs. This was one of the many ways township schools raised money and augmented inadequate government grants. It was now six years after independence from white minority rule and Angel was now in the fifth grade. Primary school education was free, but parents had to pay other individual school costs, like activity fees and building funds. The majority of primary school children in the townships, like Angel, came from very poor families who could hardly afford to feed their children, let alone pay any money to the school. So schools came up with various innovative ways to raise funds for whatever projects the school found necessary beyond basic government sponsored educational needs.

The end of school term entertainment was the highlight of Angel's school year. The magicians were his favourite performers. Luckily for him, the school always hired a magician, either because he was the most popular or because he was the cheapest.

Angel dreamt of becoming a great magician one day. While sitting in class he would often day dream about what he would do to his class teachers if he was a magician, particularly those nasty teachers well-known for caning. The day dreaming compensated for all the frustration he had to go through each day at school. The most frustrating part was sitting in class for six hours every day listening to the teachers explain things that he never seemed to understand. At each grade, teachers seemed to give up trying to make him understand anything. They looked forward to the end of the year when Angel would move on to the next grade and become the next teacher's problem.

Moving from one grade to the next did not depend on the child's performance. As long as he or she had spent the whole year in that particular grade with more than sixty percent attendance, they were considered good enough to go to the next. It was only when parents intervened and asked the school to get their child to re-do a grade that they did not do well, did performance become a factor.

Unfortunately, for most children, they were lucky if their parents even knew what grade they were in. As Angel was considered a lost cause, both the school and his mother had no interest in his performance. His mother was too busy worrying about where their next family meal would come from, paying bills and keeping their heads above water to think about her children's school grades. And so Angel resigned himself to the end of the week canings.

Every Friday, the class had a test on the material they had learnt that week. The test was marked out of ten points. For every wrong answer each child got, they would get a lash on the hand. Angel could hardly remember a week when he got less than nine lashes.

Imagining becoming a magician was also a way for Angel to escape into the fantasy world of super heroes and get away from his dire realistic situation both at home and at school. He would imagine that if he was a magician he would turn dry leaves into money for his mother. At school he imagined being able to read the test answers on the teacher's desk without having to walk the 10 metres from his to the teacher's desk.

The more time he spent in his fantasy world, the better he felt and the less time he had to see and think about the extreme poverty he was growing up in. It was the reality of township life that school children who were getting good grades were considered to have a higher chance of escaping the township poverty and were always associated with being successful later in life. They were used at school and at home as benchmarks for other children to follow. There were plenty of examples of unsuccessful school dropouts in the township who were used as an example of what not be. Most had either been in prison and back, some more than once. Others did odd jobs or were employed as labourers in the local industrial area, earning a minimum wage and spending all their earnings at the local beer garden. Alcoholism, prostitution and drug use were very common in the township where Angel was growing up. Being unsuccessful at school was highly associated with these vices later in life.

From one grade to the next, the obsession with magic stayed with him. Seeing magicians at school three times a year at the end of each term further fuelled his obsession.

The best moment for Angel came when he was in the sixth grade. He was sitting in the front row, as usual, at one of the end of term school entertainment sessions. The magician asked for a volunteer for one of his many tricks. With no one raising their hand, out of fear and superstition, the magician pointed at Angel and asked him to come on stage. After shouting "abracadabra", which was the magician's word for performing this particular trick, he pulled a string of different coloured cloths tied together from Angel's ear. From that day Angel was known at school by the nickname "bra" a shortcut for "abracadabra", a nickname that he carried all the way to the end of primary school.

During his last year of secondary education, at the age of eighteen, Themba, Angel's eldest brother, was already dreaming about leaving home and going to South Africa to work at the mines. He had heard stories told by older men in the township who had been to the South African gold mines during the Winala years. Although these people had nothing much to show for their many years in the mines, they always told rosy stories of lots of money and a great and fun life.

Winala was the popular name of the recruitment agency that was set up by the gold mining companies in South Africa to recruit migrant workers from all over southern Africa from the 1940s to the late 70s. Its real name was Witwatersrand Native Labour Association. Unfortunately, more than seven in ten of the men recruited by the agency from the townships of Bulawayo went to South Africa and never came back. This did not deter more people from joining the trek south. The migration from Matabeleland and the townships of Bulawayo in particular continued into the eighties and nineties but had shifted from just looking for work in the mines to all sectors of the economy where blacks were allowed to work.

During Themba's end of high school days, more and more young men and women were still leaving to find employment and a better life in South Africa. Some never returned or communicated with their families back home, although not as many as in the seventies. A lot more were now coming back to visit. Themba's dream was not to be one of those people who went and disappeared. He intended to come back one day with enough money to look after his mother, brothers and sister. He told his family that he would always communicate with them and let them know how he was doing.

One of Themba's school mates, George, had a
brother and an uncle who migrated to South Africa
during the Winala era. George had abandoned school
just before the last year of secondary school's final
exams and went to join his brother and uncle in
Johannesburg. This was not a unique situation, as some
young men, particularly those considered not having a
chance of doing well in their final exams, did not wait
to complete their secondary schooling but left at the
earliest opportunity.

Just over a year after George left, he had come back
to visit during the Christmas holidays. The December
holidays were generally the time when most migrant
workers came back home and they would go back in
January. It was George's new possessions, like a car,
money and never seen before electronic gadgets, that
convinced Themba that he had no other choice but to
make the journey down south if he was ever going to
live a better life. Unknown to him, the car George was
driving was a rental car, the electronic gadgets he had,
were stolen property and the money he was spending
was savings earned from mundane temporary jobs. It
had taken George the whole year to save for this
month long visit.

Soon after completing secondary school, Themba
loitered in the township doing odd jobs for more than
a year, saving and waiting for an opportunity to leave.

He hooked up with two of his friends and they paid a haulage truck driver to smuggle them into South Africa.

For nearly five years his family did not hear from him or get any information about his whereabouts. It was only after George came visiting at the end of the fifth year that Angel's mother learnt that he had made it to Johannesburg. He had lived and worked as a gardener in Khayelitsha for a year before moving to the diamond mines in Kimberley in the Northern Cape Province about 500 kilometres from Johannesburg. This was the last information she would get about him for many years to come. She never heard from Themba himself.

Life was really tough for children growing up in the townships, but it was worse for a girl child, like Sihle. The preferred option for most parents was to send their sons to school rather than their daughters, no matter how intelligent the girls were compared to the boys. For parents who could not afford to send all their children to school, the girl would rather drop out of school and give the boy a chance. This was based on the premise that girls would eventually get married and go and join their husband's family, and would not be of any financial benefit to their parents in their old age. Yet the boys would be able to find a good job and earn a lot of money and be able to look after their parents. So investing in a girl's education was viewed as a loss.

Sihle was lucky in that respect as her parents managed to pay for her primary and secondary education. This was mainly due to coming from a relatively small family. She was not one of the brightest students in her class, just like her brothers, she was not even average. Out of a class of thirty-five students, during all her primary schooling, the best she had ever done was to come out thirtieth. Like most of the other failing students, the school let Sihle continue to the next grade as long as she completed a full year at the school and had a more than a sixty percent attendance record. On her last day of primary schooling the headmaster and all her teachers where glad to see the back of her and other students they considered lost causes.

Secondary school was no different and she was no good at any sports activities either. There were not many sports activities to choose from, except athletics and netball for girls and soccer for boys. Secondary school teachers were overworked and under paid and as a result, did not have time for students who did not do well. The teacher to student ratio was even higher than at primary school level, with one teacher looking after forty-five students. Sihle did not have any incentive to go to school other than to fulfill her mother's wishes and spend time with her friends.

By the time she was doing her second year at high school she had become sexually active. The last year of secondary school was a struggle for her. The year seemed to take longer than usual and felt like a real waste of time. She preferred to be roaming night clubs in the city, getting paid to have sex with drunken men then spend the rest of the day dozing in class. She could hardly wait for the year to end. As soon as she finished writing her last school exam, she became a full time prostitute, joining a number of other township women who had been doing this for a long time.

Sihle's first child, a girl, was born a year after she left school. The man she claimed to be the father of the child refused to have anything to do with the pregnancy as he was already married and accused her of picking him as he was financially well-off compared to all the other men she had been with. The man demanded to have a paternity test after the child was born. Sihle, who was not even sure if he was really the father of the child, refused and preferred to look after the child as a single parent.

She joined the ranks of a string of other single parent women in the township who were in a similar situation. A couple of months after the child was born, Sihle was back at work, leaving her mother to look after the child. It was a tough time for the infant, who had to be looked after by the grandmother at night, and during the day her mother would be sleeping most of the time.

Two years after the child was born, Sihle had her second daughter. This time the man she claimed to be the father of the child accepted the responsibility. The man's relative came to see Sihle's mother to negotiate and make the relationship formal and go through all the traditional marriage rites. Sihle's life seemed to be taking a different direction. Her mother felt very happy that her daughter was taking a dignified direction in her life and would finally settle down.

Angel was sixteen years old and understood that his sister was better off married and in a good stable family relationship than being a lady of the night. He thought his mother and most other mothers in the township pushed their daughters to look for the wealthiest man to get married to. It did not seem to be important that the man loved their daughter or was not abusive. The main factor seemed to be good prospects of economic and social protection from men. Maybe this was a symptom of poverty. He could not understand why township women considered marriage as a lifetime achievement, something far more important than a good career or getting out of the township on the back of their own individual success.

One of the most shameful things a daughter could bring to her parents in the township was to leave her marriage. Leaving a marriage carried so much stigma that women would rather die at the hands of an abusive and violent husband than leave him.

Angel had seen women in the township who had stayed in their matrimonial homes even after the man had brought in and was living with another woman and was constantly abusing them and their children. This kind of desperate dependence on men was continuously being passed on from one generation to the next. It perpetuated a sexist and paternalistic culture that undermined the women's ability to seek economic autonomy. It also created generations of men who believed in the perverted idea that women were subservient property for men to do with as they pleased.

Sihle and her second child went to live with her new husband. The marriage did not last very long. She accused the husband of not giving her enough money to support her lifestyle and her daughters.

After five months of living with the new husband, Sihle and her daughters were back home and she was back to her old profession. Angel sensed his mother's embarrassment at the break-up of the marriage. But he felt a strange, somewhat guilty and unpleasant, sense of admiration for his sister for walking out of a marriage that did not suit her needs. He thought that because she was able to stand on her own two feet financially, even though she earned the money in an unorthodox and indecent way, this had made it easy for her to leave.

It took a lot of courage for a woman in the township to do what she did.

At the red light district, things were not the same anymore, an absence of eight months seemed like a lifetime. There were new and younger faces at the night clubs, who, to Sihle, looked far too young to be prostitutes. She remembered the days when she was young and men were falling over each other for her services. She used to joke with other prostitutes of her generation calling the older women SUBs, or substitutes. They called them so because men only asked for their services as substitutes if they could not find or afford younger women. SUBs was also their acronym for stupid, ugly and broke. They called them stupid, because they thought they must be idiots to still be in this business at their age, ugly because they had lost their youthful and beautiful looks and broke because they accepted any fee for their services.

Every time the young girls passed by she felt the pain and humiliation. She now understood how those old ladies they used to laugh at felt. Most of her generation of prostitutes, particularly her friends, had either been fortunate to find a husband and settled down, had moved to other towns or had died. Life had moved so fast and was so cruel and now it was her turn to be a SUB. Men did not seem to give her a second look and she was not making as much money as she used to. To make matters worse she felt very tired most of the time and was losing weight despite not changing her diet.

As months went by, the more weight she lost, the less men where interested in her. She had heard about sexually transmitted infections, had contracted most of them over the years. Gonorrhea, herpes and syphilis, she had been treated of them all, and in her circles, they were considered just a hazard of the job. This new disease that was now being talked about, particularly by the social worker really scared her. The social worker they called Auntie visited them now and again at the night clubs to warn them about the dangers of sexually transmitted diseases and teach them about what protection was available for them.

Sihle used protection most of the time, but some of her clients refused to use it and were even prepared to pay her extra if she agreed not to use protection. This new disease Auntie warned them about had so much stigma associated with it that no one dared mention it or agree to voluntary tests. What was particularly worrying Sihle was that she was now exhibiting most of the symptoms that the social worker had mentioned as associated with the disease.

One day, after her regular midday sleep, she was feeling too sick to go to work. That evening, she felt like she had contracted malaria; she had severe flu symptoms in addition to her usual tired and weak feeling. That night she stayed at home.

The following morning she was worse, she was sweating and very cold at the same time, had a headache, muscle aches, tiredness, nausea, vomiting and diarrhea. Her mother took her to the local clinic, where they referred her to the hospital.

After a week in hospital and different types of medication, she felt a bit better. At the end of the second week of hospitalisation, she got a surprise visit from the social worker, Auntie. After chatting to her for a few minutes, the doctor came and told her the news she was most terrified to hear. She was HIV positive, and because she had left it too late to get tested, she now had full blown AIDS. Auntie tried to comfort and counsel her, but she felt the little life and hope of recovery she had left drain out of her.

The following morning when her mother visited her, she could hardly believe how much she had deteriorated over the last couple of days. After the news, her condition took a downward turn and she never recovered. It was like she had given up on life.

Three weeks after being admitted to the hospital, Sihle died, leaving her two young daughters to be looked after by their grandmother. Ma Ncube joined a list of thousands of other grandmothers left to look after AIDS orphans.

His sister's death got Don thinking about where his own life was going. His older brother had disappeared to South Africa and now his sister was dead, that made him the eldest child in the family. He needed to step up and look after his mother, young brother and nieces.

It was now two and half year since he completed high school. There were very limited choices for black students who passed their last year of high school. They could either go to the teachers college, an apprenticeship, to nursing school or find a clerical job in one of the local companies. Further education was reserved for those who did exceptionally well as the places for advanced level education were extremely limited. For young men like Don, the door to a better future seemed to have been slammed in their faces the last day they left school.

Don felt like a lost soul, he helped his mother sell vegetables and cigarettes at the local beer place, but he was not making as much money as he needed. To get extra money he joined up with three of his former classmates, who were in a similar predicament, in shop lifting, carry out burglaries and other petty crimes. His life revolved around earning easy money and spending time with his girlfriend who was doing her last year at secondary school.

The small time criminal gang was increasing the size of their loot as they got more and more confident. Their reputation was spreading all over the township and the police were beginning to take notice. Don and his friends were always fantasising about taking their trade to South Africa.

In November of that year, just before she started writing her final exams, Don's girlfriend became pregnant but did not tell anyone, not even Don. She managed to write her exams and leave secondary school without anyone suspecting.

On Christmas day she gathered the courage to tell Don. He was devastated to hear the news. He could not see himself raising a family with the money he was making. It was the last news he wanted to hear. The police were on his trail and now he had a child on the way; his world seemed to be caving in on him.

December was the time a lot of South African migrant workers came home for the end of year holidays and returning in early January. On the third of January of the following year, Don and his three friends disappeared without telling anyone. His mother was worried sick as word circulated around the township that they had been arrested. His girlfriend's parents also sent their relatives to tell his mother that her son had got their daughter pregnant. It was one bad news after another for maNcube. She could not bear losing another child and gaining another orphan to look after.

After two weeks of agonising worry and stress, she got the news that Don and his friends were ok and living in Johannesburg. They had hitch hiked a ride off one of the many migrant workers returning to Johannesburg after their end of year holiday. Ma Ncube was greatly relieved to know that her son was alive and well, she was also glad that he left because she knew that his next destination would have been prison. She still had the coming grandchild to deal with, but that was the least of her worries.

It was now two years after he left school and Angel was desperately looking for a way to follow his brother to South Africa. The economy was slowly deteriorating and there was an increasing number of job losses due to retrenchments and company closures. A lot of people from across the country, particularly from the township, were moving to South Africa, Botswana and Namibia in desperate search for work.

Angel heard that one young man, John, who lived three blocks from his house, would be leaving for South Africa soon. He spoke to him about the two of them making the journey together, as Angel did not know how and where to go. He had heard that his brother was living in Hillbrow and had been given an address, but he had no clue where that was and how he would get there.

The two young men left on a Friday morning and boarded a rural bus that took them south west to Plumtree Town, near the Botswana boarder. From there they took another rural bus headed south to John's rural home in Brunapeg, reaching the village late in the evening. They met John's cousin, Rodney, who was going to take them across the border the next day.

At 3am on Saturday morning, they started the walk across the bushes towards the boarder. It was pitch dark and Rodney was walking too fast for the two city boys. When they left the village, Angel was feeling cold and had put on a jersey. After trying to keep pace with Rodney for half an hour, he was puffing and sweating and had to remove the jersey.

As the sun was beginning to come up, they came out of the bush tracks on to a dust road. They walked again along the road for a while and came across a small shelter. Rodney told them that this was a bus stop and they had to wait for the next bus into Francistown. Angel was surprised to find they were already in Botswana. He expected they would jump over a fence, hide from border guards or come across something that showed they were crossing a country border. It was his first time out of his home country and he had been hoping it would be much more eventful than it had been.

When they stopped at the bus stop, Angel was very tired but relieved that the walking was over. It was not long before three other people came to the bus stop. They greeted the three young men in Setswana. Angel assumed they were locals from the surrounding villages. Taking a lead from Rod, John and Angel answered the greetings in Setswana too. The bus eventually came and they paid ten pula each for the hour long journey to Francistown.

It was still early morning when they reached Francistown, but the main bus station was already a hive of activity. Rod pointed them to where they would board the bus to Gaborone, the capital city. He told them that when they got there, they were to ask for the taxis or people movers going to Mafikeng and from Mafikeng they would get a bus to Johannesburg. He was going to do his weekly shopping and head back to the village. After saying goodbye and good luck, he disappeared into the crowd.

Just before 9am, the two young men got onto the bus going to Gaborone. From the language spoken in the bus, Angel figured that the majority of the people were from Zimbabwe. As soon as he sat down in the bus, Angel fell asleep. He had woken up earlier than his usual time and had walked for miles like he had never done before, so his body could do with the sleep.

When Angel woke up and checked the time, it was just after 2 pm, the bus had travelled for over five hours. They were now in the city. The buildings in Gaborone looked well maintained, the roads were wide and had no potholes like back home. Shop windows displayed beautiful clothes, furniture and gadgets he had never seen before. The bus stopped at a traffic light. Looking at the people walking about, Angel thought people in Botswana looked happy and less worried than people back home. The bus turned left at the next intersection and into the main bus station. It was another hive of activity, much busier and more crowded than the bus station on Francistown.

They got off the bus and stood next to a line of market stalls that seemed to divide the buses from the taxis. The taxis were sixteen-seater Toyota Hiaces used for local, suburb to city travelling as well as for long distance city to city transport like back home. From the taxi ranks they could hear people calling for travellers to different cities and suburbs. They stood there listening for one calling for Mafikeng, but none was forthcoming.

Angel then heard a female voice calling his name. He did not know anyone in Botswana and wondered if they were calling someone else with a similar name. Looking at the direction where the voice was coming from, he saw a lady dressed in a white dress and white head scarf waving at him from one of the market stalls. While he was still trying to figure out who it might be, John said to him, "She's calling you, let's go and ask her where we can find the taxi to Mafikeng." He nudged Angel in the lady's direction.

"Oh, yeah," said Angel as they walked to meet the stranger.

"Hi, Angel, what are you doing in Botswana?" the lady said as she put her arms around him. "How's your mother? I am your Aunt, Joel's mother," she said as if sensing that Angel did not recognise her.

Joel was one of Angel's friends from the neighbourhood. His late father had four wives and he had so many brothers and sisters, Angel had never known how many there were or which ones were Joel's step siblings. His family were members of the Apostolic Faith sect, popularly known in the township as 'mapostori', a localised word meaning apostles. Joel's mothers and sisters always wore white dresses and white head scarves. His father and brothers always had shaved heads and long beards. During his primary school days, Angel envied Joel because he never had to go to school. The sect members did not send their children to school, they did not seek any medical attention from clinics or hospitals and they buried their dead in their backyard and not at the council cemetery. Angel and Joel did not get to play together much after Angel started secondary school, because Joel was never around anymore. He was always in the city helping at his father's shoe repair shop. It had been a long time since Angel had seen Joel or any one of his four mothers.

After digesting all these thoughts in a matter of seconds, Angel felt good that they had come across someone he knew.

"We're going to Johannesburg," said Angel in an excited voice and lit up face that showed he was talking to a familiar face.

"That's a good thing Angel; there are no jobs at home. It's better for you to try in South Africa. Do not disappear like your brothers. Make sure you remember my sister, your mother. She has gone through a lot since your father passed. I knew you were always a good kid Angel."

"Yeah, I will try my best," replied Angel, not sure what to say.

"Do not be like your friend, Jo." Which was what everyone used to call Joel. "He was getting into trouble back home. But when he came here and found a job in Mahalapye, he seemed to mature and is doing better."

"Is that where he is?" asked Angel rhetorically.

"Life is not easy in Joburg, Angel, but you must persevere, do not give up," said Joel's mother as she fetched something from her purse.

"And make sure you stay away from crime, drinking and prostitutes" she continued. "Here take this," she said, as she handed a twenty pula note to Angel. "You will find the taxis going to Lobatse and Mafikeng over there." She continued pointing in the direction of the taxis, interrupting Angel who was about to say something.

"Thank you so much," said Angel looking in the direction Joel's mother was pointing.

"Go now, boys, before it gets dark, and God bless you," she said.

John and Angel were grateful to find someone they could trust pointing them in the right direction. They hurried towards the taxi that was calling for travellers to Lobatse. They asked the conductor calling for Lobatse if he was going to Mafikeng.

"Yes it is, and its twenty pula to Mafikeng," he said excited to have two passengers at once.

"Do you have passports?" he asked lowering his voice.

"No," John quickly replied.

Angel had never owned a passport. It was too expensive for him and it took too long to get one. Besides, they would have needed more money to apply for travel visas, which they were not guaranteed to get. It was much cheaper to travel this way. They also had a higher chance of reaching Johannesburg than travelling the normal way.

"Do you have an extra thirty pula each?" asked the man.

"Yes," replied the two young men simultaneously.

"Ok, let's go," he said jumping into the taxi after them.

They were the last two passengers to make the sixteen needed for the taxi to start on its journey. It was just after 3pm when the taxi left the city. The speed limit was 120km/h, but Angel was sure the driver was travelling at far more than that.

The rest of the journey was through a desert. They passed a number of sparsely located small rural villages, but the rest was a vast land with nothing. It was different from Zimbabwe, where the vegetation featured widely scattered trees and dried grass in between. They reached Lobatse within an hour. Six people left the taxi and six new passengers jumped in. Soon they were travelling through another desert.

After travelling for about forty-five minutes, the conductor who was calling for passengers in Gaborone and Lobatse asked everyone to hand over their passports and fares as they were getting closer to the boarder. He asked Angel and John to give him fifty pula each.

At the border, the driver parked at a designated taxi area where there were a number of other taxis. He asked everyone to stay put in the taxi. He took the passports and went inside the customs and immigration building. He was in there for about an hour, and Angel and John were getting worried that something might have gone wrong when they had come so far. Angel looked into the horizon as the sun was gradually setting, what a beautiful sight at such an anxious moment, he thought. Bright yellow rays of light filtered through the dark clouds, turning dark yellow and red as it got lower towards the dark earth. While he was still lost in watching the heavens, he suddenly heard the sound of the starting engine and a door sliding close. The driver was back and they were on their way.

They drove about a hundred metres to the border crossing gate. The security guards took the passports from the driver and counted them, then counted the passengers. He looked back inside the passports and took out the twenty pula, put it in his back pocket and handed the passports back to the driver. He waved to another guard to open the gate. The taxi rolled through the gates into no man's land, then drove for about a hundred metres and stopped again at the South African side of the customs and immigration building.

The driver got out and entered the building with the passports. Angel noticed that there were fewer cars on this side of the border. The building was modern and there were security cameras on the walls. The lights, which had just come on, were far more sophisticated than the ones in Zimbabwe. It looked like he was in a completely different world altogether. This time, the driver was back quicker than he had taken on the Botswana side. Again, the security guard took the twenty pula out of the passports and handed them back to the driver. As they drove out of the gates into South Africa, Angel assumed the other twenty pula would be shared between the driver and the conductor. The driver gave the passports to the conductor who distributed them back to the passengers.

They were in South Africa now and he felt relieved. It did not matter what happened now, the road was now clear for them to get to Johannesburg. It was dark but the roads where clearly lit. They got on to a two lane highway and Angel saw a road sign showing 'Mafikeng 20 km'.

They drove at high speed like he had done while they were in Botswana. While Angel was still mesmerised by the modern and well maintained infrastructure, the taxi drove into a hotel parking area where there were two other taxis. He told the passengers that their journey ended here and those who wanted to get to the bus station for buses to Johannesburg could walk across the main road. John and Angel quickly got off the taxi and followed the driver's directions to the bus station.

There were just a few taxis left at the station and no buses. John went to one of the taxi drivers and asked which one of the taxis was going to Johannesburg or if there were any buses coming later. He was told that all buses going to Johannesburg had left and the next one would be in the morning. Taxis would not go there unless there were enough passengers to fill it up. They had to wait until either there were fourteen other passengers going to Johannesburg, which was unlikely that night, or wait until the next morning.

After waiting at the bus station for about an hour with no other passengers coming, the two young men resigned themselves to spending the night in Mafikeng. They decided to go to the hotel where the taxi from Gaborone had dropped them off to buy something to eat. They had made up their minds that they would spend the night at the bus station. They had seen a lot of other people preparing to spend the night at the station, particularly women speaking Shona. Angel was so excited to be in South Africa that he did not care about where they would sleep.

At the hotel restaurant they ordered take away and sat at a table next to the door waiting for their food. After five minutes, a young man wearing a waiter's uniform walked in, he stopped and watched John for a while like he recognised him but was not certain. John looked up to see who this stranger was, his face immediately lit up. The two smiled at each other and John stood up to greet him.

"Hi Doug, it's good to see you after such a long time," said John.

"Is it really you? You have grown so big. What are you doing here?" asked Doug, not giving John a chance to reply.

"Angel, this is Doug, my cousin Rod's best friend. Doug this is Angel my friend," said John doing the introductions.

"Pleased to meet you," said Angel as he shook Doug's hand.

"Pleased to meet you too," Doug responded, then turned back to talk to John. "I have tried several times to get Rod to come to South Africa but he's not interested. That guy loves Brunapeg like he's the mayor. The last time I saw you was, what? Four years ago? That was during the school holidays when you came to visit your grandparents."

"I was there yesterday, but just passing through, I didn't see anyone, but I heard your parents were fine," said John.

"Our food's here," interjected Angel as another waiter wearing a similar uniform to Doug's handed him two paper bags.

"Thanks," said Angel as he took both paper bags.

"You're early today, your shift doesn't start for another twenty minutes," said the waiter looking at Doug and walking away, not waiting for a reply.

"So what are you doing here?" asked Doug again.

"We're on our way to Johannesburg," John replied.

"Johannesburg? Why would you go there, you'll get shot in Joburg," said Doug jokingly.

All three of them laughed.

"You won't be able to get there tonight, so you'll have to stay at my place and go tomorrow," Doug continued, telling them, not asking.

"Are you serious? We were going to sleep at the bus station," said John.

"I only have one room, but it's better than the bus station," said Doug.

"Look, we can sit here and you can eat your food while I wait for my shift to start. One of the cleaners finishing work at ten lives next door to my room. He will take you there," Doug said looking happy that he had come to the rescue of one of his rural home boys.

Angel could hardly believe their luck. This journey was going so smooth. It must be a good omen for the rest of his life in South Africa, he thought.

After chatting for about 15 minutes about the highlights of their adventures while herding cattle in their rural home, Doug and John said good night, promising to continue their chat in the morning.

Doug rented a room in Dibate Mafikeng. Doug's work mate let Angel and John into the room and showed them where the bathroom was, then left. He lived a few blocks down the street from the house.

There was not much in the room, a single bed mattress with folded blankets on one end and a pillow on the other lay on the concrete floor at one corner of the room. On the opposite side, just behind the door, was a small table with a one plate stove, a couple of small pots and plates and some cooking utensils. Next to the mattress, on the pillow end, was a small radio cassette player with a wire attached to its antenna running out to a closed window. Above the blanket side of the mattress were some clothes hanging on a string that was attached each side of the two walls. Angel and John lay the blankets on the mattress and were in a deep sleep within half an hour.

Doug came back to his room in the morning just before seven. The two visitors were already up, they had folded the blankets as they had found them and were ready to go. Doug was excited, but this did not surprise Angel as he had been excited to see John the previous night.

"I have good news for you," said Doug looking at John.

"What news?" asked John, curious and surprised.

"One of the cleaners on our shift resigned, he got a waiter's job in Pretoria, and so I told the supervisor that I have a cousin who is looking for a job."

"Are you serious," interjected John, not sure if what he was hearing was true.

"So the supervisor said I should bring you along tonight."

"Yes, I'll go with you," replied John without giving it a second thought.

"What about our journey to Johannesburg?" Angel asked, interrupting the excitement, anxious about what would happen to him if John stayed in Mafikeng.

"You can still go to Johannesburg without John, or you can stay and look for a job here," said Doug.

"No, I have to go and stay with my brother in Johannesburg," said Angel, determined to see Don.

From the time he said good bye to his mother, he had been looking forward to meeting his brother and sending a message to his mother that he had seen him and that he was ok. He was a bit apprehensive about continuing the rest of the journey on his own, but felt that he could not let his mother down like his two older brothers. Travelling with John had given him moral support and had made the journey less uncertain.

Doug and John felt the disappointment and fear in Angel's voice. "Johannesburg is about five hours away. Why don't you go and if you don't find your brother, you can come back," said Doug.

"Ok, thanks. I have to leave now so I can get there early," said Angel, picking up his bag from the floor.

"Let's take Angel to the bus station and I'll come and tell you all about the job," said Doug to John.

The three left the room for the bus station. The early morning sun was already beating down on the dusty roads of Dibate. Angel looked around and saw a different place than he had imagined the previous night. The houses were sparsely scattered with a lot of them still under construction. They all looked different, like everyone was building their own design. Some sections had dry overgrown bushes. They walked up to the main tarred road and got a taxi into town.

The bus station was busy with taxis calling for passengers to different places. Angel said goodbye to Doug and John and got into the taxi bound for Johannesburg. The two rural homeboys did not wait for the taxi to leave, but turned and disappeared into the busy crowd. It was the last time Angel saw the two friends. The taxi waited for another four passengers before departing.

It sped into Johannesburg Park Station while Angel was still impressed by the development in the city. He had only seen such complex road networks and high rise buildings on TV. The city was all he had imagined it would be.

He soon found himself standing outside the taxi, not knowing which direction to turn. He saw some shops a small distance from where he was standing and decided he would go there and find someone he could ask for directions to Hillbrow. Outside one of the cafes was a middle-aged couple sitting, waiting to be served their food. They were speaking Shona. Knowing a bit of Shona from back home, he thought these would be the best people for him to ask. To his surprise he was not too far away from Hillbrow. The couple gave him a detailed explanation of how to get to the street that he was looking for. They told him they understood how he felt, being in a big city for the first time and not knowing where to go. They had been in his situation before. After giving him some encouragement, Angel left the couple and walked in the direction of Hillbrow.

In twenty minutes he was standing outside a dirty building that looked like it had seen better days. Outside the building in the middle of the street, vendors were selling all sorts of things. He hesitated to enter, afraid of what he might find.

"Who are you looking for?" asked one of the vendors, speaking in Zulu. She was holding an infant child and sitting in front of phone cards and other electronic gadgets.

"I am looking for my brother Don," replied Angel, wondering if that had been the correct response. Certainly this lady wouldn't know a Don in such a big city.

"You are Don's brother? You look like him," she said, somewhat surprised.

To Angel that sounded good; she knew his brother or at least someone with the same name.

"They would be sleeping in their room," she said without waiting for Angel to reply.

Angel was not sure who else she was referring to, but did not care, he was excited that he was about to see his brother.

She called one of the young men who seemed to be either one of the vendors or was just loitering around the stalls. She asked him to take Angel to Don's flat. The young man was happy to take Angel into the building. After going up the stairs to the third floor, they knocked on a slightly open door, which did not seem to have a flat number on it.

At the age of twenty-one, Angel had joined the great trek down south to Johannesburg. His imagination of glamour and a better life in South Africa soon vanished. Don and his criminal gang spent most of the day sleeping, loitering in the Hillbrow streets and drinking alcohol. They went out at night going to 'work'. Don told his brother that he worked night shifts.

Angel soon found out what working night shift meant, when on the second week after he arrived, one of Don's friends was shot dead after the gang tried to rob a house in one of Johannesburg's wealth suburbs. Angel had never seen so much blood in his entire life. The sight of blood on his brother's clothing, which had got on to him when they tried to help their fatally injured friend as they ran away from the crime scene, made Angel nauseous. As soon as the gang realised their friend was most likely going to die, they dumped his body outside the local hospital and sped away in their stolen car. They drove the car to a bushy area just outside the city and set it on fire.

Angel found out that the infrastructure in Hillbrow was so dilapidated it was worse than in his home town. It was as if Hillbrow was in another country and not in South Africa. He still hoped to make it somehow somewhere here in South Africa and did not contemplate returning back home with nothing.

He had moved into the room his brother shared with his gang of six, now five. Four of them came from Zimbabwe, including the now deceased gang member; the other two were from Mozambique. The whole building they lived in was rented out to the tenants by a Nigerian landlord, known as The Manager. He was also believed to be a drug lord who had hijacked the building from its several rightful owners. The owners dared not step into Hillbrow due to the violence and its reputation as the most dangerous suburb in the most dangerous city in the world.

The tenants in the building where living in squalor, there was no electricity, the lifts did not work and the staircase was littered with rubbish. There was a common bathroom at the end of each floor's passage way. It was not difficult to find in the darkness, all one had to do was follow the stench.

One morning, as Angel ventured out of the room, he stepped over someone lying on the staircase between the first and second floor, either fast asleep, too drunk or dead. He did not stop to find out. Out in the street, there were so many people and vendors everywhere selling all sorts of items, from phone cards, fruits to belts and cellphones. His brother had told him not to go too far from their room and avoid anyone looking like a policeman. If he came into contact with a policeman he better have R50 to bribe them to let him go, otherwise he would find himself getting deported back to Zimbabwe for not possessing the correct papers to be in South Africa. He was told to learn to speak with a South African accent and learn the names of rural South Africa as soon as possible, as the police identified foreigners from local migrant workers by their accent and the lack of knowledge of rural South Africa. His brother had warned him to walk away from any trouble if he could, or else he better have a gun or at least a knife as this neighborhood was rough and violent. In the meantime, Don was going to organise him fake identity papers.

Angel soon realised he had to find his own feet and get out of Hillbrow as soon as he could or else he would find himself in prison, deported or worse.

His brother helped him get fake South African identity papers, and he was soon out and about looking for employment. It took him about three months to pick the correct accent and know half of the names of rural KwaZulu Natal, which he would use as his cover story if caught by police. Coming from KwaZulu Natal was the easiest and most convincing cover story for most Zimbabweans coming for Matabeleland. This was because the Ndebele kingdom, based in Matabeleland, which was first led by Mzilkazi and later by Lobengula originated from Zululand after the demise of King Shaka. So most surnames were the same and the languages had a lot of similarities.

Don and his gang never seemed to run out of money; they were always driving a different stolen car and the police were always looking for them. When they were not out robbing rich people, they would be out partying in the township shebeens. Although Angel did not take to drinking alcohol or smoking cigarettes, he always joined the gang when they visited the townships of Soweto. This is where he met other young Zimbabwean men in similar situations and made friends. Instead of spending all his time in Hillbrow, Angel was now able to spend time in Soweto, squatting with friends, mostly from Zimbabwe, Mozambique and South Africa.

Employment was not easy to come by, so he still depended a lot on his brother's blood money to survive. His passion for magic was still burning and he was hoping to get an opportunity to perform magic part time even after he got a permanent job.

Chapter 2: Life in Johannesburg

Angel used some of the money he got from his brother to take private lessons in becoming a professional magician from Blair Leon, a mixed race graduate from the College of Magic.

He met Blair one night when his brother took him to one of the city nightclubs where Blair was performing. He approached the magician during his performance breaks to find out how he ended up in this career. He was delighted when Blair told him that he could teach him the trade for a small fee.

Blair ran a private unregistered school of magic from his two bedroom home in Alexandra's middle class area. His class had three students, two who resided at the shanty town part of Alexandra, and Karlos Dube who stayed with Blair. Angel became the fourth student, and he was of no fixed abode. He drifted between Alexandra, Hillbrow and Naledi in Soweto.

Blair was a small time magician who took his students around the township schools for magic performances. He also performed at one of Johannesburg's nightclubs every Saturday night. His four students would assist him at his performances as part of their lessons. Angel's keen interest and the quick way he mastered the tricks really impressed Blair. At some of the school performances, Angel was allowed to lead the way and be the main attraction. This gave him the confidence and the joy he had always dreamt of when he was a child watching magicians perform at his primary school. Still, he was not making any money from this and had to pay Blair R50 a month for his training.

Karlos and Blair met during Blair's glorious days as a champion swimmer in Cape Town. Karlos was a potential professional swimmer who was doing very well at school swimming competitions. After leaving school having failed his metric, Karlos became friends with Blair through their common swimming interest.

Rumours about Blair's sexuality had been brewing for some time. When the swimming club that he represented heard about his suspected gay relationship with Karlos, he was confronted about it. He confirmed that he was interested in men but denied having a relationship with the young Karlos. The club unceremoniously dismissed him as other members of the club and his swimming partners became uncomfortable associating with him.

This fall from grace drove him to become an alcoholic; he was rejected by most of the members of his family who could not accept his coming out of the closet. No other swimming club was prepared to accept him. After spending time at an alcohol rehabilitation centre, he left the sport altogether, moved from Cape Town to Johannesburg and started a career as a magician.

Seeing what Blair had gone through, Karlos decided not to pursue a career as a swimmer. He subsequently left Cape Town and joined his friend in Johannesburg. The two, however, continued to be frequent visitors to the local public swimming pool where no one knew who they were.

The other two students, Fred and Godfrey, had been street kids in the Johannesburg streets for some time before meeting Blair. Fred came from Durban; he was raised by his single mother who died when he was five years old. He was adopted by a very abusive uncle. When he was ten he ran away from home. Scared that his uncle would find him in Durban, he hitched a ride on a goods train that took him to the streets of Johannesburg. For six years he survived sleeping rough and eating from the dumpsters. He met and made friends with another street kid, Godfrey.

Godfrey came from Musina and ended up on the streets of Johannesburg at the age of eleven. His father died when he was an infant. His mother remarried when he was five, but he never got along with his stepfather. After six years of a turbulent life that seemed to get worse every year, he stole his parents' savings and left home for good. It did not take long for the money to run out. After roaming the streets for three years, he met Fred, who became a brother he never had.

Coming from similar circumstances, the two teens met when dumpster diving behind a city nightclub. Because of the good and fresh food that the nightclub threw away, they became regular visitors to these dust bins. The club manager and employees got to know them well as being good young men. Soon they were being asked to do odd jobs around the club, like help performers carry their gear in and out of the club in return for food. They took a keen interest in the performances of one of the nightclub's frequent performers, a mixed race magician known as Blair, who was always accompanied by a boy just a little older than them.

The next five years saw the two friends' lives gradually change. They became Blair's magic students and made another two good and close friends, Angel and Karlos. They moved to Alexandra and found a shack to call home.

One Sunday afternoon, Angel left Alexandra where he had spent the night after a Saturday night magic performance, and arrived in Hillbrow as he had done on many occasions. Sunday was a good day to come to Hillbrow and see his brother, spend a couple of nights and get some money to sustain his drifting from Soweto to Alexandra the rest of the week. But today was different, the building where his brother's gang lived was being cleared of all the tenants by a private security company. People wearing orange overalls were helping residents clear their belonging. Heavily armed police stood by in case of any trouble, and another group of police officers went among the tenants checking for identity papers with a police van parked just a few metres from the building loading all tenants suspected of being illegal emigrants.

The retaking of the hijacked building on behalf of their owners by private security companies in conjunction with regular heavily armed police officers was nothing new in some parts of the city. But it was a new thing in this part of Hillbrow, which was considered long forgotten and abandoned. Angel was more concerned about his brother's whereabouts. He was not worried about bumping into any police officers, as his fake identity, South African accent and a convincing story of coming from Kwazulu Natal had proved several times to get him out of trouble. In any case, he still had some money to bribe his way out if he was threatened with deportation.

He walked around the crowd of onlookers, hoping to see someone from the third floor and ask if they had seen his brother. It had been just over two and a half years since he arrived in this suburb of Johannesburg and he was now a well-known face among the long term residents of Hillbrow. As he walked around the stunned crowd, he came across Lizzy, one of the long term tenants of the building who had a vending business at the corner of the street. Her corner stall sold mostly stolen goods brought to her by the different gangs that resided in this and the neighbouring buildings. She also had a well-known prostitution ring operating from one of the hijacked flats in the same building where Angel's brother lived. She knew Angel and Don very well as Don was one of her regular clients. Angel realised that she was looking excitedly keen to talk to him as he approached her.

Heavily armed police had come early that morning; they entered the building, while the private security company guards surrounded the building to make sure no one escaped. The police had gone from floor to floor looking for wanted criminals and asking everyone else to get out of the building. This is when Don and his gang got arrested; they had no time to escape. After arresting all the known criminals, other residents were allowed to go back into the building to collect all their belongings. They had to reenter floor by floor, starting from the top floor but accompanied by the orange clothed guards. They were told to leave the building and never come back. Any valuable thing that was left behind was removed or looted by the guards. The rest was loaded into waiting rubbish trucks and taken to the city's land fill.

Angel's small belongings that had been in his brother's room were also taken to the rubbish dump. He realised that this was the end of his life in Hillbrow; the next thought that came to his mind was to find out where his brother had been taken.

As he stood in the midst of Johannesburg, he found his thoughts drifting back home to Zimbabwe. He thought about his mother, and the pain she would feel if her second son was to disappear like the first one. He thought about how he had come to South Africa with such high hopes for a better life, only to find himself without a job and homeless. Even though this place had been a filthy hole, and he did not spend much of his time here, the fact that this was where he had always come when he had nowhere else to go made it feel like home. Now they were being evicted and his only relative was now in prison. As all these thoughts raced through his head, he was oblivious to the scenario unfolding in front of him. When he came back to his senses, he asked Lizzy the question that was worrying him the most, where did they take his brother?

She told Angel that all those arrested had been taken to Yeoville police station. She had seen these criminal gangs get arrested, go to jail and come back to continue their business so many times. Some of them never even made it to courts. They just bribed their way out of the system. Lizzy was street smart, she knew the lawyers that would readily represent the gang members for the right fee. If Angel had the money, Don would not even make it to court. These lawyers could make the docket disappear from the police station by paying the station chief. But Angel did not have that kind of money; however, he did have enough to go to Yeoville police station to see his brother.

When he arrived at Yeoville police station, things unfolded as Lizzy had said. The first police officer Angel came into contact with at the station asked if he was here to bail out his brother and how much money he had. Since he did not have any money to bail out his brother, Don and his gang where going to go to court sometime during the week to answer for their many crimes. If he wanted to see or know where his brother was he could always come back to the police station any time. After satisfying himself of his brother's whereabouts, the next thing on Angel's mind was where he was going to stay. Going back to Alexandra for the night was his first option. He thought about going to Soweto, but he felt much closer to his Alexandra friends, since he would have to ask if he could stay with them indefinitely.

Angel's arrival at his friends' shack in Alexandra did not surprise Fred and Godfrey. The story he told them about the raid in Hillbrow, his eviction and his brother's arrest was interesting but not unfamiliar. They had seen this several times during their days in the streets. These raids happened here too. Alexandra's shanty town was also full of criminal gangs that often got raided by armed police and private security companies. Fred and Godfrey did not object to Angel living with them. They had grown up homeless and knew what it was like not to have a place to go and lay your head every night. This was the new South Africa under Thabo Mbeki where, for those at the very bottom of the economic ladder, the different with apartheid South Africa was the ANC's empty promises.

Life in Alexandra was much worse than back home in Bulawayo. The shack he now shared with his two friends had no electricity or any form of sanitation system. There was only a handful of communal water taps. The communal toilets were just a hole dug into the ground inside a tin shed. People preferred to use the bush than use those toilets. The place was overcrowded and disease was rampant. All this was now apparent to Angel as he was now spending most of his time here. Every now and then he would visit his friends in Soweto. Compared to life in Alexandra, they were living in luxury. There were no schools in Alexandra, so children from the shacks went to schools in the surrounding better neighbourhoods of Alexandra. Those few adults who were employed went to different parts of the city to work while some spent most of the day begging in the city centre, particularly at the main bus and train station.

A month after Don's arrest, he was sentenced to five years in prison and incarcerated at the Johannesburg prison. At least Angel knew where to find his brother for the next four years, that is, if they did not move him to another prison. He promised his mother, whom he was always in touch with, that he would visit his brother at least once a month and tell her how he was doing.

The first time Angel visited Don was two weeks after his sentencing. He had already been beaten twice by the guards and by other inmates. It was his first time in prison for such a long period. Jail was not a strange place to him as he had been arrested several times since he had come to South Africa. But on all previous occasions he had served his time, the longest of which was three weeks, in the local township prison.

Johannesburg prison life was tough and dangerous. Here there were more hardened and more vicious prisoners than Don. The prison gangs made his Hillbrow based criminal gang look like a bunch of altar servers. The only consolation was that for the next four years, he had a roof over his head and three square meals a day. Angel was really afraid that his brother would not survive his sentence.

After a year in Alexandra, Angel's life wasn't showing any signs of improving, instead it was going from bad to worse. He feared for his life as rumours were circulating that his friends and him were involved in homosexuality and witchcraft activities. This suspicion had been fueled by their relationship with their magician mentor Blair Leon. It was an open secret in the township that Blair was living with Karlos as his gay partner.

The three friends, all Blair's students, lived in fear. They were being taunted and called names if they were seen walking together in the neighbourhood. There was one particular old man, Sam, who used to bask in the sun outside one of the many shanty town tuck shops. Old man Sam did not mince his words, when he saw any one of them, he would ask them why they were practicing homosexuality. The three young men always denied this, but that did not stop Sam from asking the question every time he saw them. He wanted to know why boys their age didn't have any girlfriends or why he'd never seen any one of them visit one of the many local well-known prostitutes in the area. He asked them why they spent so much time with the coloured (mixed race) homosexual, Blair, if they were not like him. He even offered to get them girlfriends if they were too shy to ask or pay for any prostitute they fancied. But the young men would just laugh it off.

Angel used to enjoy chatting to old man Sam as he found conversations with him direct and amusing. He was the go-to man for any news happening around the shanty town. He was amazed at how much the old man new about what was happening in and around the shanty town, even though he never did much except bask in the sun outside the tuck shops all day every day. He would find it funny when Angel tried to explain to him that he was not gay but was waiting to meet the right girl before getting married. He found it even more hilarious that he thought visiting prostitutes was wrong and dangerous because of the HIV infection. Old man Sam would tell Angel about how, as a young man, he worked in the gold mines around Johannesburg, drank heavily and visited prostitutes every time, but not once did he get sick or get infected with HIV. Angel would reply saying, there were no cell phones during that time either; life was very different now. It was old man Sam who would later save Angel's life.

One Sunday morning in the shanty town of Alexandra, a pastor from one of the many local Pentecostal churches gave a sermon about how the Bible condemns homosexuality. He quoted a number of Bible verses to justify his preaching. Leviticus 18:22 "Do not have sexual relations with a man as one does with a woman, It is a detestable sin." 1 Corinthians 6:9-11. "Don't you realise that those who do wrong will not inherit the Kingdom of God?...Those who indulge in sexual sin,...or practice homosexuality ... none of these will inherit the Kingdom of God." Jude 7 – "And don't forget Sodom and Gomorrah and their neighbouring towns, which were filled with immorality and every kind of sexual perversion. Those cities were destroyed by fire and serve as a warning of the eternal fire of God's judgment".

Using the last quote from Jude, the pastor incited the congregation to get rid of all semblance of homosexuality from their neighborhood, otherwise they would burn in hell and fire just like Sodom and Gomorrah.

By the end of that Sunday afternoon, word had spread around the neighbourhood that the three young men who are always seen in the company of the coloured man must be burnt in their shack while they slept in order to save the rest of the neighbourhood from the wrath of God.

Early the next morning, as Angel walked past the tuck shop, old man Sam waved at him to come and talk to him. As Angel got closer, Sam looked around to make sure no one else was listening; he quickly whispered to Angel to get out of Alexandra and never come back. He put a R20 note into Angel's pocket and said goodbye, tapping him on the shoulder.

Although confused and terrified, Angel felt the seriousness of the warning and did not ask too many questions. He knew things where really bad as Sam had never given him or anyone any money ever.

Angel ran east to the edge of the shanty town. He ran across the bushes adjacent to the Jukskei River to the nearest main road and jumped into the next available taxi. He sat in the taxi for 20 minutes, terror visible in his eyes and his heart pounding like it wanted to escape from his chest. He sat there in the taxi so absent-minded that he didn't hear the taxi driver asking him if he was ok as he looked like he had just seen a ghost.

The taxi driver dropped Angel off as close as possible to Blair's house, at 23 Pitt Street, Alexandra West. Although he was not sure exactly why he had to run, Angel had a strong suspicion that either a xenophobic or homophobic attack had been planned and he must have been the target. He tried without success to call his two friends on their cell phones to warn them that something was wrong and they needed to get out of Alexandra.

Blair and Karlos immediately realised that something was not right as soon as they set eyes on Angel. They had never seen such fear in his eyes. His hands were shaking and he could not hold the glass of water Karlos had just given him. The thought of having been so close to death made his whole body feel cold. He had heard in Soweto how people, suspected of being police informants, were burnt alive during the apartheid days. He had also seen videos of foreigners in Cape Town being locked in shacks and burnt alive in xenophobic attacks. He hoped that someone had warned his friends just as old man Sam had warned him. He knew people in South African townships did not accept homosexuals and he had heard stories of some gay people being raped and killed. But he did not think that people in the Alexandra really believed that his friends and him were gay.

He remembered how Fred was always talking about one of the bar maids at the night club; he was hoping to ask her to be his girlfriend one day when his life was in order. Angel wondered, if the reason their lives were in danger was not homophobic then it must be xenophobia. It had happened before in other areas of the country where foreigners were set upon by local South Africans, beaten, stabbed and burnt alive just because they were immigrants. They were accused of taking jobs from the locals and committing crimes like robberies hijackings and murder. All sorts of thoughts were turning in Angel's head. He even thought about how he could make his way back home if his situation got worse.

The next morning, the news was all over the radios and television, two homosexual men had been burnt alive in a shack in Alexandra.

Nine months after being evicted from Hillbrow, Angel was homeless once more. He had escaped the shanty town with only the clothes he was wearing. The little that he had in the shack was now burnt to ashes. For the first time since he had arrived in South Africa, he seriously considered going back to Bulawayo. He would need at least R500 to get back home. He checked his pocket and the only money he had was the R20 Sam had shoved in his pocket. Looking at the money made his thoughts drift to old man Sam, knowing he might never be able to see him again. Going back to the shanty town would be suicidal.

As he sat alone outside Blair's house, he found himself shedding tears for his friends who had given him shelter; they had been like brothers to him all these years. What pained him most was that he knew that they were good people trying to find their way and build a life in an environment that had all odds stacked against them. They had lived very difficult lives and died a very cruel and vicious death for no good reason. More tears rolled down his cheeks. His friends had suffered so much, they did not deserve to die in this manner. He had never felt so much pain in his heart since Sihle's death. He wished he had died with his friends. He wanted so much to talk to his mother in Bulawayo, but did not have enough air time on his phone, nor did he have the money to purchase any. He thought life could not get any worse.

Listening to talk show radio that morning made the whole incident even more painful. Most South Africans who phone in expressed support for the actions of the people who had burnt down the shack. The DJ was calling for someone from Alexandra to phone in and explain why they did what they did. After about half an hour into the talk show a resident from the shanty town, who surprisingly did not support the actions of his neighbours, phoned in. She wanted to remain anonymous and explained how generally homosexuals are hated in the area, just like in most communities in South Africa. This had never translated in to murder before until this past Sunday when the local preacher, whom she mentioned by name, had passionately preached about destroying homosexuality in the community. As these three young men had always been suspected to be gay, they were targeted for destruction. She did not know how the third one survived or where he was, as he had apparently disappeared from the neighbourhood.

Angel was absolutely terrified as he listened to the radio. She was asked if the police were investigating the death of the two and disappearance of the third person. She said the police had not been to the scene yet and she did not expect them. They did not bother to investigate any other crimes committed in the area let alone homophobic ones. Within the ranks of the police force, some shared the same view that gays should be burnt to death.

Police turned up three days after the incident to remove the remains of the dead men and ask questions about the murders. That was the last time anyone heard anything about the case.

Angel's thoughts turned to his current situation, where was he going to live? He had spent the night at Blair's house. The next alternative would be to try and stay with his Zimbabwean friends in Naledi. Blair considered Angel his brightest and most promising student; he invited him to stay at his house. In exchange, he would have to find more magic performances and start earning enough to pay for his stay. His magic skills had improved so much that he was able to run his own shows. Blair also told Angel about his relationship with Karlos. He confirmed that the rumours in the shanty town were correct about him and Karlos being gay. Angel was still too shocked about his escape and the death of his friends to care about other people's sexuality, besides he already knew.

The residents of this part of Alexandra did not care about what their neighbours did as long as it did not interfere with their own lives. There was also better security in this area from private security companies and police investigated crimes committed in this neighbourhood. So Angel was safe here. Since Blair and Karlos shared a bedroom, Angel had his own bedroom. For the first time in his life he had a bed to himself in a room where he slept on his own. He was given some of Karlos' old clothes to wear and started rebuilding his life.

Blair subcontracted to Angel his contract to perform magic at the primary school on Diepsloot. The contract was for performing at the end of term event, which meant performing four times a year. The R300 paid for these performances was enough to pay Blair for the accommodation in Alexandra.

Angel was so much loved by the kids that they spoke about him everywhere, to their parents and neighbours. Soon his name was known to the whole community. He used the attention he got from the kids while performing magic to educate them on other social issues, like staying away from drugs, alcohol and crime during their school holidays. His strategy of integrating magic entertainment tricks into engaging in purposeful conversation with the students impressed the teachers. It was something Blair had never done. Angel had never deliberately set out to do this but it just came naturally to him, he felt that just entertaining the students was not enough; they had to get something out of the whole experience. It gave him so much joy to see the smiles on these children's faces, even if it was just for an hour. This was one of the very few moments of happiness that they would get, as most of these children would be going home to a shack with no electricity, no running water and they would be lucky if they would have something decent to eat.

As his reputation spread, he started getting invitations to perform at other community events, including election political rallies and governmental and non-governmental social gatherings. Any event in Diepsloot that needed to draw a large number of young people always featured Angel's magic show in its programme.

Angel's mixture of magic and learning was so successful that the teachers decided to invite him during the school term to help with some of their most difficult subjects. This was good for Angel as he did what he loved and made some extra money from it.

From the Diepsloot end of school term contract, casual lessons and weekend nightclub magic shows, he was now making more regular income than he had ever made in his life. Although he was getting very busy, he never missed his monthly visit to the Johannesburg prison and was now able to send some of the money to his mother in Bulawayo.

Angel used a number of different magic tricks, depending on his audience, taking care not to perform the same tricks too often. His keen interest in magic and the training he received from Blair were paying off. He even included some of his own dramatic effects around magic tricks. Some of his tricks included pulling a white rabbit out of a black hat. This he did using a specially rigged table with a rabbit compartment, a black hat with an opening top and a well-trained rabbit from Blair's rabbit cages. He would show the audience the empty hat rolling it around to show that there was nothing in it. He then puts it on the table with the top of the hat on the table. He put his hand inside the hat, his hand going through the hat top and the table to the secret compartment grabbing the rabbit and pulling it up as if it was coming out of the hat.

Another well liked magic trick was the disappearing of a piece of cloth, which was done using a silk piece of cloth and a rubber thumb tip which was the same colour as Angel's thumb.

The disappearing coloured egg trick was a favourite of those students who liked being part of the show. The egg reappeared in the pocket of one of the people in the audience who then got R10 for being the lucky one to have the egg. This was achieved with the help of an assistant, in most cases it would be Karlos. Angel used two identically coloured egg-like balls. While he fooled the audience by slipping it under the sleeves of his long sleeved jacket, Karlos would have identified someone within the audience wearing loose clothes to slip the other ball into their pocket. This was like reverse pick pocketing. Angel then invited the audience to look for the egg in their pockets for a R10 reward. Kids loved this trick, the excitement of the prospect of being chosen to magically have the egg as well as getting to keep the money.

Another simple but very entertaining trick was cutting and restoring a piece of rope, where Angel cut a piece of rope which then appeared to be magically restored. This involved the introduction of a short piece of rope of the same type as the main longer one, and cutting that instead, then bringing back the main longer rope. He played around with the ropes in such a way that the audience never noticed that there were two different ropes.

Other magic tricks Angel was well known for were the vanishing coin; the ring moving up a string defying gravity; putting a white cloth in a glass, then completely covering the glass and magically removing the cloth out of the glass while the glass was still covered; and levitating a pen in an empty coke bottle which he achieved by using a near invisible fishing twine attached to the pen and his belt.

One of Angel's most amazing but rarely performed magic tricks was that of walking on water. The trick was mainly reserved for high dollar paying audiences, large audiences and nightclub special occasions.

Chapter 3: Angelbert the Preacher

The headmaster at Diepsloot School was really impressed with the way Angel engaged his students, particularly the way he managed to get any message across to them. He thought he would be an ideal person to talk to the youth at his local church, the Christ's Happiness Gospel Church (CHG). He was now in his second year working with the school. After the performance of the last school term the headmaster invited Angel to come and join him at their next Sunday church service. Angel decided it was good business to keep a good relationship with his client and hence accepted the invitation. Angel tried to invite both Karlos and Blair to come with him, but they refused, saying that most of the churches were the biggest source of discrimination against gays.

Angel enjoyed his first day at the CHG church so much that he became a regular attendant and helped the headmaster with his youth programs. The church pastor was very impressed by Angel's gift of capturing the youth's attention and getting them to understand whatever he was talking about. He was also intrigued by how Angel introduced magic tricks to get their attention if they seemed to be losing interest.

At the end of one Sunday service, the pastor called him aside and asked him to stop using magic at his church. He had a proposal Angel could not refuse as it involved getting paid. If Angel joined the church as a youth leader, he would be paid a regular weekly wage. His job would involve talking to and running the youth programme every Sunday. The headmaster had recommended Angel for the job as he thought Angel was able to do a better job than him. Angel would also take part in membership recruitment events for the church. He had to promise that he was not going to perform magic at any of the church events as this activity had not been sanctioned by the church's leaders.

It was not long before Angel's recruitment skills and his ability to draw crowds came to the attention of the head of the CHG church, Pastor Josphat Jabulani (JJ) Zulu.

JJ was based at the church's headquarters in Jabulani, Soweto. He started the evangelical church eight years earlier in Soweto. Before that, he was a deacon at the Zion Christian Church (ZCC) in the Limpopo province. One night coming from preaching at a rural Limpopo ZCC outpost, he was involved in a near fatal car accident and spent forty days in a coma. He spent another three months in hospital after coming out of the coma. During these three months, JJ had spent most the time watching free-to-air Christian channels. He saw how other pastors in America, United Kingdom, Nigeria and South Korea were gaining so much wealth preaching the gospel of prosperity. He had known about prosperity gospel preachers his entire career, but had never paid much attention to them. He watched with amazement at their popularity, celebrity status and how large their churches and crowds where. He watched with admiration Nigerian preachers like Bishop Opedeyo of The Conquerors Synagogue, Pastor Olomide of The Embassy of Jesus and David Petomite of The Church of Nazareth. He was impressed by American evangelical preachers like Benny Hin, Joel Meyer, Joyce Mayor and Chris Dollar.

On his release from the hospital, JJ was totally convinced that he had to follow in the footsteps of these rich pastors. He believed that his accident was not just a simple accident, but a sign from God for him to move in this direction of worship. His time in hospital had given him the opportunity to reflect on where his life was coming from and where it should go. He now sincerely believed that he had received a revelation from God while he was in a coma, telling him to go to Soweto and start a new prosperity gospel church.

Soon after leaving hospital, JJ resigned from his position at ZCC. He sold all his possessions, took the insurance money from his accident and moved with his whole family to Soweto. He preached that his recovery had been a miracle and that he had died and gone to heaven. God had told him to come back to Earth and save the people of Soweto and beyond from poverty and internal damnation.

JJ moved his newly founded CHG church doctrine away from the ZCC traditional Christian doctrine. He instead focused on the Word of Faith doctrine, promising his followers health, prosperity and happiness. His Word of Faith preaching encouraged his followers to flaunt their wealth as a sign of God's favour. He told them that they should hold up their material possessions as proof of God's gifts to them for their faith. He told them that they must show their gratitude by donating a tenth of it to the church or else God would be unhappy and would take their wealth and make them poorer than they had ever been.

His church had grown slower that he had expected over the past eight years. His audience had not reached the same numbers as other overseas preachers he'd seen while in hospital. He had grown into six branches across Johannesburg, mainly based in townships and shanty towns. His total congregation was a couple of thousand, with the largest at his base in Jabulani.

JJ had found that prosperity gospel was more effective when preached among the very poor. The more he flaunted his money and put a show of being a wealthy pastor, the more poor people he attracted. He found that these people were taken in by a combination of trust in him and any other person who preached the word of God as well as the hope to gain the riches promised by JJ's message.

Traditional gospel concepts preach that it is easy for a camel to walk through the eye of a needle than for a rich man to enter the kingdom of God, Mathew 19:23-24. The traditional message did not reconcile wealth and faith. Yet there was JJ and other word of faith preachers saying the rich are rich because they are faithful to God. That God is here for mankind and to give mankind wealth, health and happiness. That it was actually easier for the rich man to enter the kingdom of God than traditionally thought. Here was a new doctrine from this charismatic, smartly dressed man of God that teaches of true religious fellowship. He taught that good behaviour and giving to God leads to material prosperity and he had the wealth to prove it. Suddenly, poor people had found a religion that resonated with their aspiration of great financial prosperity and personal success as an expected evidence of God's favour.

JJ took the view that in order for his church to grow and match the likes of Nigerian and American prophets he had seen on television, he would have to recruit other charismatic preachers who shared his ideas. He was always on the lookout for talented charismatic preachers to join his church, and what he had heard about Angel seemed to fit in well with that criterion.

When he found out from the pastor at his Diepsloot church that Angel had only taken up the offer of leading the youth for a fee, JJ knew this was one person he could easily recruit into his church if he was the great communicator he had been said to be.

When JJ visited the Diepsloot branch, he came with his entourage of shiny cars, well dressed body guards and state of the art sound system, the church was packed. His visit had been advertised and marketed well in advance. Angel was instantly impressed by this man. He had heard about him, but in the flesh, he surpassed his reputation. He was even more impressed by his message. Although he had heard the same concept from the local pastor, this man put the message across with more eloquence. He laced it with Bible scripture right through the three hour long sermon. By the end of the sermon, Angel could not believe how even the most impoverished people he knew in this shanty town where falling over themselves to be seen giving a donation.

Angel was surprised and delighted to hear the news that JJ wanted to have a private meeting with him. He was very excited to be able to meet with the leader of the CHG church and the pastor who rose 'from the dead'.

JJ told him that he had heard about the good things he was doing for the church and for God. How the congregation had grown, particularly the youth, since he joined the church and it was time for his faith to be rewarded with riches as true to the teachings of the church.

He invited Angel to come and join him at his Jabulani headquarters. He said he had great future plans for him. He would be given a fully furnished house, a car and would be rewarded with more money the bigger the church grew. One thing JJ said to Angel that stuck in his mind for ever was that Christ's Happiness Gospel (CHG) was a business first and church second.

This was an offer Angel could not refuse, he had come to South Africa seeking riches and his dream was coming true, although this was not how he anticipated it would be. This was the opportunity he got and he was not letting it go. By the end of that week, he had packed his belongings from Blair's house and was moving into his new three bedroom house, with furniture he had only dreamt of. He felt happiness and pleasure to be going to the new place but also a slight feeling of sadness to be leaving Blair's house, particularly leaving Karlos.

He was given a car and a driver while he learnt how to drive and get his own driver's license. He had never had the money or the opportunity to get one before. His mother always told him and his brothers when they were growing up that if they ever got a chance to drive a car, they must never drink and drive. She told them that they must remember that their father died because of a drunken driver. She compared a car in the hands of a drunken driver to a loaded gun in the hands of a baboon. Angel assumed she used this analogy either because she meant it or she did not want them to forget, or both. Angel had never forgotten, but he thought his brother, Don, had either forgotten or chosen to ignore their mother's advice. Angel never imagined that the day would ever come when he would have a choice to drink and drive or not to.

He set about learning how to preach in front of large crowds with conviction and charisma. Every week day was spent reading, understanding and memorising the Bible. All evenings were spent in front of other trainee pastors and JJ himself, practising how to preach.

This was a different setup from magician training. He felt like he was back in school, but this time he was learning with a sense of purpose. He had a very convincing and strong incentive to achieve his goals — money. At school, he had struggled to retain information, he had never passed any memory test, but now the stakes were too high to fail. The way he captured and remembered Bible verses and was able to relate these in a long preaching session surprised Angel himself. He realised that all those years spent struggling in the classroom were not because he was stupid or dull, but that he lacked the maturity and a very compelling reason for why he had to learn and understand all those concepts.

This time he had found something to be passionate about and his mind retained scriptures like a sponge retaining water. He was dull and stupid at mathematics, geography and science, but he was a genius at magic, the Bible and preaching.

A year had passed so quickly since Angel joined the CHG and moved to Jabulani, and his transformation had been nothing but remarkable. He was able to hold a congregation's captive attention during his preaching. They would not stop talking about how his words had touched them. They said he preached like he knew what was going on in their lives. Pastor JJ was even amazed at how Angel was able to defend any argument against or in support of the CHG church, quoting multiple Bible verses. He was so eloquent at preaching a point of view and justifying his reasoning using scriptures both from the old and New Testament. JJ was sure that Angel was a great investment and he did what he did out of conviction and was not driven by money. And so it seemed. If he was able to convince JJ, he was now ready for prime time

One Saturday afternoon, Pastor JJ asked for a volunteer from among his trainees who would like to give the main sermon at one of their church branches in Bloemfontein. They were making a special visit to this church to pray for and support the local pastor who had not been feeling well for some time. Angel promptly raised his hand and Pastor JJ did not hesitate in letting him prepare for the sermon. The theme of the teaching would be about doing good things as human beings.

"The greatest things we can do for each other are the smallest, like smiling and greeting people when they least expect it," said Angel as he began his sermon in a church filled to capacity. "I am talking about things any one of us are capable of doing. Small acts of kindness, like offering a helping hand to others, relatives, friends and strangers wherever and whenever we can. This is Paul's teachings in his letter to the Hebrews. He says in Hebrews 13:1-2 'Let brotherly love continue. Do not neglect to show hospitality to strangers, for thereby some have entertained angels unawares.'"

There was not even any standing room left. The Bloemfontein council building that was hired every Sunday for CHG sermons was not always full. But this was a special day when JJ had brought his own entourage to come and perform 'miracles'. His visit had been highly publicised and he was known to perform 'great miracles' every time he visited one of his churches. Today the church was filled with regular worshippers, other members who no were no longer actively coming every Sunday and curious people from the surrounding communities.

"Imagine what a pleasant world this would be if for every act of kindness that we gave to others, they go and do the same to another, if each and every one of us found more satisfaction in giving than in receiving, if we all found happiness in being polite and courteous to others rather than being angry and vengeful," Angel continued. "The Earth would be a much better place if only we were ready and willing to forgive those who do us wrong, if only we were ready and willing to say sorry to those that we wrong, if only we all lived by Jesus's words and the golden rule in Luke 6:31 when he says 'Treat others the same way you want them to treat you'. God forgives us and does not treat us according to our behaviour. In Psalms 103:10 King David tells us that God does not treat us as our sins deserve or repay us according to our iniquities. Also, in 1 John 1:19, the son of Zebedee and disciple of Jesus says, 'The Lord is faithful and just and will forgive us our sins and purify us from all unrighteousness.' We have all witnessed how little kids play with each other and we can learn great lessons in forgiveness from them. When they hurt each other while playing they are unhappy for a few minutes and after that they are back playing together as if nothing happened. That, my brothers and sisters, is true forgiveness.

"What are other acts of kindness that we can do in our daily lives? Saying good morning to a stranger and not just those people you know. Offering a seat to an elderly person on the bus or train, listening to others when they are talking and never seeking to be the one with the last word in a dispute, offering food to the homeless and hungry and supporting the church's charity programs. The son of Zebedee and disciple of Jesus tells us again in his letter in 1 John 3:17 that 'whoever has the world's goods, and sees his brother in need and closes his heart against him, how does the love of God abide in him?' And Paul, another great disciple of Jesus, in his letter to the Galatians, 6:10 he teaches us that 'if we have therefore opportunity, let us do good unto all men, especially unto them who are in the family of faith.'"

Angel went on with his message for two and half hours, with loud punctuations of "amen" from the crowd. Occasionally some would stand up and raise their arms and shout acknowledgement that the words had touched them. Some of the people in the crowd were part of JJ's entourage, hired to mix with the crowd and carry out these performances.

Angel's last words at the end of the preaching were "Remember my brothers and sisters in Jesus, as you leave this place live by His words in John 13:34-35 'So now I am giving you a new commandment: Love each other. Just as I have loved you, you should love each other. Your love for one another will prove to the world that you are my disciples.'"

When Angel had completed his preaching, the band started playing a gospel track with the followers singing along before JJ took over and continued the day's proceedings.

The CHG and Pastor JJ in particular rationalised the church's theology model using biblical justifications. At first Angel was not sure if Pastor JJ actually believed what he was teaching or if he was just a very charismatic and pathological liar who jived with his followers as a means to an end. Either way, he was making money, lots of money by South African standards.

To Angel, whether JJ believed what he was preaching or if he was just a liar was irrelevant. Pastor JJ had plenty of examples to justify his church's prosperity gospel, like the book of Deuteronomy, which promised believers that, if they remain faithful to God's commands, they will receive numerous benefits. The book of Psalms, 37:4, also assured believers that, "delight yourself in the Lord, and he will give you the desires of your heart." He even quoted Jesus himself in Matthew 6:33: "Seek the Kingdom of God above all else, and live righteously, and he will give you everything you need". JJ said these things included food, drink and clothes to wear, that is, all prosperity. In Matthew 6:26, he says, "Look at the birds of the air; they do not sow or reap or store away in barns, and yet your heavenly Father feeds them. Are you not much more valuable than they are?"

The charismatic pastor was very convincing in his preaching and had no hesitation in believing that the Bible consistently taught that believers must trust in God's providence. To Angel, Pastor JJ was a living example of the Bible's promise in Job 36:11: "If they obey and serve him, they will spend the rest of their days in prosperity and their years in contentment".

He encouraged his followers to read for themselves the book Malachi 3:10. "Bring all the tithes into the storehouse so there will be enough food in my Temple. If you do," says the LORD of Heaven's Armies, "I will open the windows of heaven for you. I will pour out a blessing so great you won't have enough room to take it in! Try it! Put me to the test!"

He would say if they doubted his message, they must put the Lord to the test by tithing ten percent of their monthly or weekly salaries to the CHG church.

The question of where his prosperity came from was always answered by that it did not come from the church. It came from the various businesses the pastor had invested in. Since no one but the pastor himself was accountable for the church's various fund sources, like tithing, church collection, ticket sales for conferences, selling of miracle water and food, the sale of the church's books and other memorabilia. No one would know if the money invested in those various businesses originally came from those various church funding sources. All the money raised through church activities were tax free, as the church was a registered charity entity.

When Angel asked the pastor why so many people were attracted to the church and believed in this brand of theology the pastor told him that as a church and as preachers they had to take advantage of these people's feeling of desperation, either for something to believe in or a better life than they currently have. "They must fuel their hope that they too can get the riches and flaunt them just as the pastor does. That is why it is important to show off this prosperity. They must have faith in God, faith in the Bible, faith in you and your teachings. Give them the feeling that they are very important and that membership to the CHG church is the gateway to letting God give them prosperity. That it is a privilege that everyone must aspire to. The pastor must seek to redirect their feelings of desperation to a feeling of comfort in the church. We have to take advantage of their belief in God and the Bible to play fast and loose with the gospel to achieve our aims. We have to give them Bible quotations that rationalise and justify our teachings. Once they trust us and are in the state of totally believing in our position they have lost the benefit of a critical mind that could help them rationalise all this in any other context. Once we have them in this state of mind we can be as arrogant as we want, display our riches in the most extravagant way, sin as much as we want and they will still believe in us and continue to give us the little money they have."

Pastor JJ would say, "Look, Angel, we have to use our God given oratory skills to make money, remember the old Ndebele adage (Ilifa lezithutha lidliwa ngabahlakaniphileyo) 'the inheritance of the morons will be consumed by those who are clever'. We are the clever ones, they are the morons. And they will always be here since there is one born every minute. There is truth in the things that we preach but if it were all totally true, all men and women of God, bishops, pastors, priests, nuns, deacons, imams, mullahs, sheiks, ayatollahs, monks and rabbis would be the richest people in the world. All the violent thugs, con men, world dictators, prostitutes, pimps, notorious drug lords, corrupt businessmen, child traffickers and thieves would be the poorest. And everyone knows that is not the case. There are also Bible verses that we do not mention, like 1 Timothy 6:9 which says, 'But they that will be rich fall into temptation and a snare, and into many foolish and hurtful lusts, which drown men in destruction and perdition', or Hebrews 13:5 that says, 'Keep your lives free from the love of money and be content with what you have, because God has said, 'Never will I leave you; never will I forsake you.'''

The pastor encouraged Angel to spend as much time as possible reading and understanding the Bible from all perspectives. This was the only weapon he would need to counter any arguments and justify their prosperity theology. He was not going to let him become a full time preacher with his own branch unless he had thoroughly learnt The Good Book. He must be able to preach to the congregation with conviction and authority if he was to gain their trust.

JJ told Angel that he had to thoroughly understand the other side of the argument against prosperity gospel. The verses that he had quoted to support the prosperity gospel theology that referred to God's providence and all the other "materials" given to those who had faith in God were actually refereeing to spiritual providence and not necessarily earthly materials.

"The best way to improve and defend our position is to study and know the counter argument. Take for instance, you will be constantly asked how you can display and spend so much wealth when some people around us are so poor, homeless and can hardly afford a meal. Quote Jesus's own words, in Mark 14:7: 'You will always have the poor among you, and you can help them whenever you want to'. Tell the critics that we do help the poor. This is the very reason why we have to gain maximum publicity for the charity work that we do. To achieve the best visibility we jump at highly publicised cases of desperate people and not only come to their rescue but be seen to do so. We only give opportunistic charity donations. Our helping hand is only a means to an end. Every donation is like a marketing business deal, it must result in a win-win outcome both for the beneficiary and the church. The bigger the win for the church the better. The more we are known for the good things we do the better our chances of defending our positions and recruiting new members. Remember every new member is a new potential source of revenue.

"Angel, you must know that there will always be people who are prepared to follow any charismatic leader, be it for political, religious or any other perceived commonly shared ideology. People believed in and followed Hitler, Stalin, apartheid, even Satan himself. The vast majority of human beings are hard wired to seek leadership and belong to a group, especially when it is an exclusive group. And once they belong to the group and feel like they share a common interest with the other members, they are more likely to do things they otherwise would not have done as individuals.

"The desire to belong and believe in what others in the same group believe in overshadows their capacity to rationalise their actions individually. The CHG Church is providing these people with the opportunity to be a member of an exclusive group at a price. And as long as they are members of the church they will donate the little money they have, money they would not have donated without the benefit of herd mentality.

"There are many ways to make them feel that they are part of the CHG family, like visiting their homes, sponsoring theirs and their children's church weddings, using our political and business connections to find them employment and even burying their dead. If these people did not belong to our church and donate money to us, there would be someone else ready to take advantage of them and take their money. There would be other super rich pastors, charlatan and evangelical hustlers prepared to take our place and make millions of dollars by twisting the bible's message to these ignorant, gullible and readily available givers.

"There is no difference between us taking these people's money and the traditional churches whose pastors abuse their children and adulterate with their wives. I am cognisant that not all traditional churches exploit their congregations, at the same time it is not all the evangelical pastors who are in it for the money.

"In the grand scheme of things, we live in a world of exploitation of one man by another. The western world has grown rich at the expense of colonising the third world. The rich are rich at the expense of those that have worked for them, while they pay them just enough to survive and come back tomorrow and work again. This is business, Angel, our product is God and our value proposition is hope."

"Put yourself in the eye of God, Angel, and imagine watching the Earth from far away in the universe. What do you see?" asked JJ. Without giving Angel the opportunity to answer he continued. "I see this bunch of ants who cannot get along, they seem to spend the little time they have chasing the most useless of worldly things. For the little time they have on Earth, they seem to behave as if they will be here forever. I only have to rotate the Earth around the sun sixty times and the life of an average human is over. Only half of that time, as they spend the other half sleeping, is all they have to do the best for themselves, their fellow men and their next generations. But what do they do? They disobey all the ten commandments I gave them, they fight wars, kill each other, abuse drugs, exploit each other for money, you name it, they have done it. They have even become creative at sinning. Because of their self-centered individual greed, they have exploited their only home to the point of jeopardising they own existence. Each individual is trying to reap the greatest benefit for himself and his tiny group from the dwindling resources without regard for the welfare of the Earth or the next generations. It is a commons dilemma down there. They go around their business like the Earth is invisible. Surprisingly, fear brings them together. When their collective existence is immediately and directly threatened, they forget their differences and work together. Amongst them, I see the best and the worst."

"Now come back down to earth and put yourself in my shoes, Angel, I have already had more than fifty rotations around the sun. I have two choices: I can either waste the remaining ten working for others or let others work for me. I have chosen the latter. And by joining me, my son, you have wisely chosen to let others work for you. Remember the words of the preacher, Ecclesiastes 1:1-5: 'Meaningless! Utterly meaningless! Everything is meaningless. What do people gain from all their labour at which they toil under the sun? Generations come and generations go, but the earth remains forever. The sun rises and the sun sets and hurries back to where it rises'. If all the toiling is meaningless, let others do the work for us."

Did this mean that JJ really believed in the Bible? Or did he selectively believe the parts that were expedient for his aims? Angel thought to himself.

JJ continued talking, "The majority of people let events shape their lives rather than take the initiative and shape events around their lives. Then when events around them are bad they blame others and take no responsibility for their inaction. When all chips are going south, they come to us, again expecting somebody else to do something about their situation. That is exactly what we do, promise them miraculous fulfillment of their desires for a fee. Those who take the initiative and shape events around themselves are either very successful or complete failures. But it is better to try, fail and learn from your mistakes than spend your short life wondering what it would have been if you tried or blaming others for your inactions."

"But how long can these people keep giving before they realise there is nothing for them?" asked Angel.

JJ continued, "After years of giving and hoping, most of them are financially worse off and disillusioned. They either just leave the church or find another rationale to justify their more miserable status. By then they would have served their purpose to us and we would have moved on to recruit new members. They do not expect to get their money back as there are no refunds for giving to charity. This is the very reason why we invest the money that we get from them and also drive to recruit new members all the time.

"There are basically two reasons why we invest these donations. First so that it is not apparent that we are spending the church's money. Second, it is also illegal and unethical to directly convert charity donations for our own personal use, but there is nothing in the law that says we cannot invest it and live on the profits. Moreover, the businesses that we invest in are not church properties, but our personal private companies.

"Remember, Angel, this is a business first and a church second. Our policy is money first and gospel second, that is why we have lawyers, and business and financial advisors on our payroll. This whole thing is a very successful tax free business. The model is found all over the world, in Brazil, America and Asia. It is not an accident that we, the Word of Faith preachers, have massive followings. We wear expensive clothes, live in mansions, drive luxurious cars, and some of us even own private jets, which I am aspiring to, by the way. Selling God is a very profitable business. This is the life you are destined for Angel, and I can prophesy that."

"Pastor JJ, you are always accurate with your prophesies so I am glad you have had that prediction, but how do you do that?" Angel wanted to know.

"I am happy you think so Angel," said JJ with a smile of satisfaction. "Besides our oratory skills, charisma and manipulating Bible verses, belief in prophesies are one of our most important value propositions.

"Prophesies are nothing more than calculated guesses based on good information about the issues that we decide to predict. It's not entirely true that I am always correct, in fact my success rate is probably three times out of a hundred. We aggressively publicise those I get right, this makes it appears like I am always right.

"We have an information gathering and analysis team within the church that looks for information about different issues, particularly those issues people are most interested in. The more information we can get, the stronger our chances of applying deductive reasoning and the greater our chances of being accurate. We pay a lot of money to the government intelligence community to get this information. The thing to remember, Angel, is that people do not usually remember ninety-seven percent of predictions that do not come true because they are suckers for those that do come true. They will follow you to the ends of the earth if you predicted the death of a politician they all wish was dead.

"Take for instance a simple fact like predicting lottery winnings. We know that a majority of people who come to our church conventions and revivals are poor and they buy lottery tickets. So all I have to do is prophesy that they will win the lottery without being specific about whom I am referring to. And I only do this within large gatherings to increase the probability. So everyone who has a lottery ticket thinks I am referring to them. If they win, my prophesy has come true, if they do not then they assume I was not referring to them. If no one in the crowd wins no one remembers my prophesy. But if one person wins, then we encourage them to tell others so that my prophetic powers are confirmed.

"I can predict the impending death of a country's president, all I have to do is listen for rumours of a sick president in the news or any other sources. Then we send a word to our intelligence contacts to dig more in that direction. They will tell us the cost of paying intelligence sources of the country in question, who in turn pay the president's doctors or nurses or any other person who has access to his medical records for the information. Everyone has a price, especially government employees. Since we do not use this information to harm anyone, it's not hard to get. We do not even need the actual date of possible death, we can do well with just the first or second half of the year. Just know that their condition is so bad that death is imminent, is good enough to make us prophets. Putting all this information together we can prophesy without mentioning the actual country or the president's name but just give a hint in the right direction.

"The Bible is full of warnings of false prophets, Matthew 7:15, Acts 13:6 and 2 Peter 2:1, just to mention a few; we are here to fulfill that Bible warning. Still, people will believe what they want to believe and if they are paying for it we will deliver. We do not force anyone to join our church or donate their money; we just convince them to do so. We are no different from any other business that advertises their products and convince people to buy them only to find out later they are not as useful as touted. Also, politicians promise voters all sorts of things only to disappear after they are voted into office, but then people are still stupid enough to believe them and give them their vote again at the next election."

Pastor JJ wasn't done with the lecture. He seemed to take pleasure in explaining all this to Angel. So he continued.

"Thanks to Granville Oral Roberts and the seed-faith theology, we are able to financially benefit and prosper from the gospel and miracle healings without feeling guilty about it."

Angel questioned how the pastor was able to heal people through his faith.

"It's like magic," said Pastor JJ.

Angel could feel the hairs on the back of his neck stand up. For the first time he saw his destiny come before him. His love for magic when he was a small kid was all leading to this. This is what he was born to do. Although he was still confused as he remembered that the Diepsloot pastor had forbidden any magic performances in any events associated with the church.

"But the Pastor at Diepsloot forbids any magic performances at the church," said Angel.

Pastor JJ confirmed that this was true for any ordinary magic tricks that had not been analysed and concluded to enhance and justify the church's theology. That was the reason why only he, JJ, and a selected few pastors were the only people allowed to perform magic tricks, also known as 'miracles'.

"It has to look like a miracle, otherwise our followers would not be able to believe that there was a difference between magic and 'miracles'. Miracles are an essential part of the success of the word of faith theology in general and our church in particular. They are critical in convincing those who are sitting on the fence and hesitating to join the church."

Angel narrated to the pastor the history of his love and passion for magic. Starting from the time he was at school, how much he learnt from the magician Blair, how he performed in front of paying audiences and how that led to him joining the CHG church. Pastor JJ was delighted to find out that his new recruit was not only a great preacher but he was also an accomplished magician. It was a talent the church was definitely going to benefit from.

Chapter 4: Miracles and magic

Angel's skills developed and he became JJ's most trusted sidekick. There were only two pastors sanctioned to perform high level 'miracles' within the church, Pastor JJ and Angel. The rest of the other pastors only went as far as issuing predictions, also known as prophesying and some low level 'miracles', like making 'miracle' water, oil and food.

All miracles and prophesying were staged managed from Pastor JJ's office. Only carefully studied and researched events which had a high probability of occurring were released for prophesying and each pastor took a turn to issue one. The big events, like tragic events and deaths of political leaders were only preserved for senior pastors like JJ and Angel.

Tragic events were predicted far more than good events. This was because tragedy attracted the attention of more people and was more likely to be remembered. Pastor JJ compared this to two news channels, one dedicated to reporting good events and one to tragic ones. The one dedicated to good things that happened among us would have far less viewers than the one dedicated to tragic things.

All pastors were allowed and encouraged to sell 'miracle' water and oil. They were also allowed to pray for barren women to conceive. The church took advantage of the misconception within the majority of their uneducated members who believed that it was always the woman's fault if a couple could not have children. Only senior pastors could make the 'disabled walk', the 'deaf hear' and the 'blind see'. These were only done at specially choreographed crusades or gatherings where people paid a small fee to enter. In areas where the church attracted large audiences, crusades would be organised for two or three nights.

The introduction of Angel into 'miracle' performing abilities saw the introduction of 'miracle' money. That is, money suddenly appearing in people's pockets at church events. This was one of the crowd pulling 'miracles' that put Angel at the top of the Christ's Happiness Gospel Church. With Angel at the front of most of these paid gatherings, the church's membership grew at a rate Pastor JJ had only dreamt of. The more people that came to these 'miracle' vigils, the faster the word spread and the more the crowds gathered to the church's events. For Pastor JJ, the proof of success was in the bank accounts, which were swelling faster than his belly.

To Angel, the 'miracle' of money suddenly appearing in people's pockets was simple but very effective. He had convinced Pastor JJ that to make money he had to spend some. Each pastor was asked to identify the most poor within his church, who would spread the word if they suddenly found a small fortune in their pockets. The choice of these people was to maximise publicity for the so-called 'miracle' while spending very little, which to the poor person receiving the money would be a lot.

To achieve this 'miracle' a small group of former pickpockets were paid to put the known amount of money into these chosen individuals' pockets. This was done either during the crowded entrance to the events or during the time when people were called to the front of the stage so that the pastor could pray for them. When it was time for Angel to perform the money 'miracle' he would continue his prayers as normal while looking out at known places within the crowd for signs from the two to three pickpocket coordinators as to whether the assigned pockets had been filled. Angel would then dramatise the praying for the 'miracle' in the name of Jesus to have "money appear in the pockets of believers", pointing at the crowd and asking them to search their pockets. After finding the money, the chosen individuals could not contain their excitement, they fell down on their knees and thanked Pastor Angel while showing off the money to the rest of the crowd. The whole church would erupt with excitement as more and more people found their 'miracle money'.

To make it more dramatic and genuine, the hired pickpockets and other trusted church members also jumped for joy, displaying bank notes that they had 'suddenly' found in their pockets. The large number of people who appeared to have received the 'miracle money' convinced those who did not get it that it was a genuine miracle and that it was a matter of time before it was their turn. As the excitement died down, Angel also assured those who did not receive the 'miracle' that they must not despair, their turn was coming and they would be getting even more, as long as they believed and keep giving to the church.

Stage-managed healings where done at every crusade, sometimes called revivals or vigils. These events reminded Angel of the whole night church crusades that his sister used to take him to when they were kids. In most cases, these were done at night and would run until the early hours of the morning. They involved hired actors who pretended to be suffering from all sorts of illnesses like blindness, overweight, high blood pressure or deafness.

JJ, or the leading pastor at that event, would put his hand on their head, pray using all the dramatic effects, loud voice, looking up to the heavens, shaking his head, eyes closed and jumping up and down. The actor would then collapse on the floor and twitch like they had been electrocuted. They would then lay still for a while and when they got up all of a sudden they had been healed. The actor testified in front of a mesmerised and believing crowd that they had been healed and could now see the world for the first time if they were blind. They would fall on their knees and thank the pastor for his healing powers.

At every healing, the opportunity was never missed to encourage the crowd to donate money. JJ's favourite words while the crowd was taking in the just occurred miracle were, "If the blind can see, you can also get you illness cured, your marital problems washed away, your employment problems solved and your loved one's grave sickness cured. If you believe, and if today you plant the seed by giving to Jesus that R10 you have under the mattress, that R50 you keep in the corner of your wardrobe or that R100 you keep in the bank. Give it now to Jesus and show that you want all your problems solved."

The idea, as JJ explained to Angel, was that within the crowd there was a very high probability that there were people with all those mentioned issues and they would most likely have money in their wardrobe, or under their mattress or in the bank. By mentioning all this they would feel like he was talking directly to them. For all these problems and burdens that people are carrying around, what was R10, R50 or R100 if they believed their problems could be solved?

This trick was obviously working as JJ used it all the time and the bank account reflected the success. The so-called healing of the 'disabled', 'blind' and 'barren' was a tried, tested and working strategy. Almost every prosperity gospel pastor was using it. Angel had seen this before when he was a kid and he had seen how JJ and his other pastors in the church were effectively using it. He wanted to introduce something new. Something that would tip over the skeptics to their side. Something that other prosperity gospel churches were not doing. Just like any business competing in the market place, to stay ahead and beat the competition, they needed to invent something different, something that was missing in the prosperity gospel space. Angel was already an accomplished magician, he needed to maximise this skill into something the church could use to its advantage. It was a skill that the other prosperity gospel preachers did not have.

Angel was fast becoming the darling of the Christ Happiness Gospel followers. Since he became a full time preacher, prophet and miracle worker, the audience in their Jabulani branch had grown so large they were now hiring the bigger council premises for their weekly services. The tickets to their crusades throughout the country were always sold out within the first three to four days. The pastors in all the other branches were lining up to invite him to their churches. Pulling the crowd meant pulling the dollars.

Pastor JJ, now called Bishop JJ the spiritual father, by all the other pastors, including Angel, loved it. Angel was connecting well with all generations and was attracting the most valuable age group for the church — the youth. This generation, according to Bishop JJ, was the future of the church. Their money earning power was big and would be around for some time, sustaining and growing the church, and they could easily attract their peers to join the church.

Encouraging marriage within the church was one way to keeping followers. Anyone who wanted to get married outside the church would be encouraged to get their partner to join first. JJ was prepared to spend money on lavish weddings for church members as a way to keep them giving to the church and attracting relatives of the newlyweds.

The question of marriage was one JJ always avoided bringing up with Angel. He was now the most eligible bachelor in the organisation at age 29. JJ was also worried about rumours of Angel's past life and about his two friends who had been burnt to death in the shanty town. Most people in South Africa and within the church knew about the two 'gay men' who were burnt alive in Alexandra. Just a handful of highly placed people within the church knew about Angel's connection to the fire. As time passed, Angel still showed no signs of interest in women.

Bishop JJ had ambitions to expand the church to other countries and saw an opportunity in Zimbabwe. He spoke to Angel about expanding the Church to Zimbabwe in the near future. He told him that he was the right person to take this challenge. But to portray a respectable image, they needed a family man to start the new venture. The Bishop wanted Angel to find a wife, get married in the church and if possible, have a child before his move to Zimbabwe.

This development worried Angel, besides his feelings for Karlos before he left Blair's house, he had never thought of or had had any affectionate feelings for another person, male or female. He was not sure where to start; he was not comfortable talking to JJ or other pastors about this issue in case he said something that may portray him in the wrong light.

Pastor Angel's connection to the youth had propelled him to being chief youth counsellor at the church's Jabulani headquarters. He was very successful at giving effective advice that got a lot of the youth, both church members and non-members, out of trouble. His skill saw him work more and more with the local police and social workers. Every success story gave him a feeling of happiness and satisfaction. He could relate well with most of their problems as he had experienced them himself.

Young married couples made up the second highest number of people coming to see Angel for counselling. It was a common trait to have an increase in the number of couples coming for counselling during the first week of the month. Most of them had similar issues, monetary irresponsibility turned into marital problems. The stories were very similar, the men got paid at the end of the month and then spent most of the money on drinking alcohol at night clubs with their girlfriends. When it was time to pay the bills and buy food for the family, there was nothing left. Arguments with the wife would then follow and this sometimes turned into fist fights.

To Angel, these were familiar stories that reminded him of his time growing up in the townships of Bulawayo. Domestic violence was, in most cases, related to alcohol abuse and poverty.

He recalled that, as a small kid, of all the thirty-six households in the township area he lived in, there were less than ten, where they had never seen the husband and wife physically fighting. Although as kids they were never told about some of the gruesome results of these fights, he remembered one family where the mother had died after a domestic violence incident. But at the funeral the official word was that she had died of a heart attack. The husband was never arrested but rumours continued to circulate that he had killed her. The husband later got remarried, and the new wife never got along with the two step children, she physically and mentally abused them. They were later sent to live with their grandmother in the rural areas.

Reporting these domestic violence incidents to the police was a catch 22 for most women. If they got the husband charged and jailed, he would most likely lose his job, either because of having a criminal record or being absent from work without leave. The family could lose its main and only source of income. So the majority never bothered to report. The few who did had to deal with male police officers as there were very few, if any, female police officers then. The male police officers' first question would be 'what did you do to provoke him?'

Domestic violence was not considered a police matter, unless there was very serious injury or death. The sad part was that as children many times they overheard the abused women talk about being beaten by their spouses as a sign of love. Any woman who did not get a black eye or a broken rib every now and again was viewed as not being loved enough to make their husband jealous. Angel always wondered whether this was a coping mechanism, a misguided cultural concept or if they truly believed it.

It was in one of the many counselling sessions that Angel met two young ladies. One of them, Lucy Khumalo, was a well-known regular member of the church. She had got married within the church a couple of years back at one of the church financed weddings. The other one was a new face Angel had never seen before, her name was Anna Mbeki. She was introduced by Lucy as one of her childhood friends, former school mate and her maid of honour. Apparently she was one of the brightest girls in her class and had got a job as a secretary at a law firm in the city soon after completing her matric.

Lucy envied Anna's success and high life, expensive dresses and the many different expensive cars she was always seen in. As one of the average girls in her class, Lucy had struggled with getting employment after completing secondary school. She had worked as a domestic worker since leaving school, until she got married to one of the men in the church. The church had given them a wedding they could only dream of, complete with the nice dress, bridesmaids, big wedding cake, hundreds of guests and a honeymoon holiday in Cape Town. So when her depressed friend, Anna, came to her with her predicament, Lucy did not hesitate to bring her to the church for counselling.

Anna, now aged 25, was introduced to a life of binge drinking and partying by her work mates soon after she joined the law firm. The last four years of her life had revolved around work and partying. She lived and enjoyed a life of heavy drinking at parties and nightclubs.

It was common for her and her work mates to get so drunk at parties to the point of passing out. Sometimes she woke up in the morning at a stranger's house and did not remember a thing about what had happened the previous night. At the law firm, this was something to be proud of. This was until recently, when one of the ladies at the office, 29 year old Tracy, was diagnosed with HIV. She resigned from her post to go and deal with the illness. In her farewell speech, she reflected on her life and the mistakes she had made and how she thought she contracted the disease. She said what everyone in the office had suspected but dared not say, that their life of binge drinking, partying and sleeping with strangers was the probable cause. This ushered in a time of sober reflection in the office.

For Lucy, reflecting on her life brought about a wave of regrets and depression. To make matters worse, she found out that she was now pregnant. Without a steady boyfriend, she could not tell who the father was. It could have been any one of the strangers at the last two parties, or one of the many married men she escorted to nightclubs or any one of the boyfriends she dated on and off. Even though Tracy had encouraged her colleagues to get tested, Anna was too terrified to go for an HIV test as she thought there would be a very high chance that she would be positive. This was not her only problem; she realised that she would have to bring up a child on her own on her small salary.

With all chips seemingly down, Anna went to the only true friend she had known since they were small kids, to tell her about her predicament. On hearing her story, Lucy realised that her envy of Anna's expensive clothes and luxury cars had been very misplaced. She felt very fortunate to be in her position. Even her friend kept telling her she wished she had a life like hers.

At the counselling session, when Lucy had left the counselling room, Angel kept quiet while Anna narrated her story. It sounded more like a life time confession. For some moments during the conversation, Angel felt like he was talking to Sihle. He struggled to keep the tears from his eyes as he remembered how his own late sister had lived and died just like the story he was listening to.

Anna concluded, "I am looking for a way out of my situation."

Angel replied without giving his words a second thought. "Do you accept Jesus as your personal saviour?" These were well rehearsed words.

"Yes," replied Anna without hesitation.

"For Jesus to help you with your personal problems, let us kneel down and pray," Angel continued.

Angel and Anna continued their counselling and prayer sessions twice a week for three months. Anna had now become a full member of the CHG Church. During this period, Angel was also grappling with his own predicament of how he would find a wife, get married and have a family before moving to start a new branch in his homeland.

One day after the end of a counselling session with Anna, the two walked out of Angel's counselling office where they met the Bishop. He made a comment about how Angel and Anna seemed to get along well and that Anna would one day make a good wife for a lucky man. Suddenly Angel thought, this was a God sent moment.

That night he thought hard about what he had to do next. He came up with a plan to ask Anna if she would be his wife. He would accept her pregnancy as his, and this way both their predicaments would be solved.

At their next counselling session he was very nervous and he prayed that she didn't reject his proposal.

Angel gathered his courage and asked Anna if she would be his wife. He laid out his plan, emphasising that this would be a great arrangement to get Anna out her situation, that it would give her and the child good financial support as well as a stable home and family environment. It would offer Anna a new life far away where people did not know her history. Although he did not mention it, it would also fulfill the conditions set by JJ for him to be given the green light and all the support he needed to start the Zimbabwe branch of the CHG Church. Anna said she needed time to think about it.

It was two days after their talk when Anna came back to him with a reply. She had convinced herself that this was the solution that she had been praying for. She told him that she accepted his proposal.

JJ reluctantly accepted Angel's choice because he thought the two had not known each other long enough. He was also worried about Anna's background and reputation and he doubted if the relationship was based on mutual love or it was just an opportunistic arrangement.

Nevertheless, a big church wedding was organised, and exactly five months after they met, Angel and Anna were married. It was one of the church's biggest and most extravagant weddings. Church members had to buy tickets to attend and all were sold out in one day. All those who missed out could still purchase a DVD from the church after the wedding. There were seven lucky couples chosen to be the bridal party. Anna chose Lucy to be her maid of honour and Angel asked the headmaster from Diepsloot primary school who first introduced him to the church to be his best man.

It was a typical South African church wedding. The bride wore a white dress that looked like it cost a million rands, while the bridesmaids wore pink dresses. The men wore black tuxedos and Angel wore a light brown designer suit. Church members went out of their way to show off their bling too. They competed with each other to show off who would give the newlyweds the best wedding present. All Anna's relatives, parents, brothers, sisters, cousins and grandparents were all at the wedding. None of Angel's blood relatives were present. He invited all his friends from Naledi.

There was dancing, partying and endless eating and drinking for two days. Bishop JJ told everyone that this kind of wedding was just part of what the church offered to those who planted a lot of seeds, that is, donated a lot of money. The couple was given a week long honeymoon to the Seychelles by one of the church's rich businessman.

After the wedding, Anna quit her job at the law firm and moved into Angel's house. She was now back to a life of plenty, it was like she never left her life of bling. She was back into luxury cars and could now afford all the expensive clothes without having to work for them. To top it all, her doctor told her that her pregnancy was normal and she was HIV negative. She sincerely believed that her prayers had been answered.

Lucy could not help it but feel jealous once more. She thought, how could her friend who had sinned so much, was in so much trouble a few months back, have it all once again, much more than she had. She had got a bigger wedding, better honeymoon and even a better husband. She felt that her friend had got off lightly and had even been rewarded for sinning. She wished she had left her to suffer a bit more before introducing her to the church.

As Angel's profile grew so did the membership of the church across the country. Members loved and hung onto his 'accurate prophecies' and 'miracles'. The growth of membership translated to the growth of the church's revenues. Bishop JJ put into action a plan to market Angel's name in Zimbabwe in preparation for his move. In his new assignment he would be known as 'Prophet' Angel. Bishop JJ and Angel where the only pastors who would be referred to as prophets with JJ also having the title of spiritual father. Bishop JJ's long term plan was to have one leading pastor in each country being referred to as the prophet and the rest of the pastors as just that. Angel and JJ were the only two people allowed to announce 'big prophesies' and perform the most visible and marketable 'big miracles'.

They were the only two people who were known to be able perform the 'miracle' of walking on water. This was one of Angel's bright ideas from his magic days. It was one of the many magic tricks he introduced to the church to stay ahead of the competition.

The walking on water 'miracle' went like this. A giant, white, rectangular bath tub was used, the same used during baptism ceremonies. It was five metres long by two metres wide and a metre deep. It had a set of four steps on one end to walk up and into the tub, and another set to walk up and out on the opposite end. The tub was then rigged with half a metre wide, 100 millimetre thick clear strong glass. It was placed a centimetre or so below the water surface when the tub was filled and it was filled to the brink. The glass was supported by three strong glass pillars which stretched the length of the tub on one edge. It was strong enough for full grown men to walk on. Because it was slightly submerged it could not be seen even from the nearest front row of the church or hall which was about ten metres away.

During the service, the tub was filled with 'holy water' and situated at the front of the church were everyone could see it. The edge with the rigged glass was placed towards the crowd. During baptism, the pastor stood outside the tub away from the rigged glass. People being baptised walked into the water from the right hand side of the pastor. He then used his right hand to lower their head under the water and then brings them back up. They then walked off the tub from the left. The baptism created the illusion that there was nothing but water in the whole tub.

At the end of the baptism either Angel or JJ, depending on who would be 'walking on water' during that event, made his dramatic entrance preaching and acting like he was possessed by the 'holy spirit'. At the height of the sermon, he walked up the step to the top of the tub and walked across the glass to the other end of the tub. As he stepped off the tub after 'walking on water' believers went into a frenzy, raising their hands, shouting and some were falling to the ground. They were totally convinced that their pastor was a real 'miracle' worker and true 'prophet' and whatever he said must be believed.

Angel had joined the church attracted by the prospects of making a lot of money. He got more than he bargained for. He got a lot of money and the power to influence. As he got deeper and deeper into it, reading and quoting the bible and using it as justification for their deceptions, he turned into believing that maybe he was really called by God.

He began to believe God had destined him to do His work and become a true prophet. The sheer number of people who seemed to be amazed at his work convinced him that he had divine powers. He knew that a lot of testimonies about his and JJ's healing powers proclaimed by people at their sermons were staged. What surprised him was that other people who were not part of the faked testimonies were coming out to say they or their relatives had been healed by his prayers. Some even testified that they had been HIV positive but after Angel prayed for them, they had become HIV negative. Others said after receiving his blessing and prayers they had found employment and other had been promoted to higher job positions. There were countless others whose prayers had been answered. Some women testified that they had conceived babies after Angel's prayers. He was hearing people who believed and testified that bad spirits that had haunted them since they were born, had been cast away by Angel's power and prayer.

Thinking back about his life when he was growing up in the township, they hardly had enough food to eat. He thought about his suffering when he came to South Africa and living in the dingy and dangerous flats in Hillbrow. He considered it a miracle in itself that he was now living such a life. He was travelling in the best and latest cars with an entourage of workers and bodyguards. He was meeting the who's who in society anywhere in the world, particularly in Southern Africa, and was flying only first class whenever he travelled by air. It must have been divine intervention that had got him there. It must have been God himself who had given him so much from so little.

He believed that they had to continue to use all sorts of trickery to convince people to join and remain within the church. He also believed that JJ and he had some divine powers and were real prophets of God. Whatever they decided must never be questioned, questioning their authority would be tantamount to questioning the will of God.

Unfortunately for Angel, somewhere at the back of his mind there was a persistent little nagging thought that questioned his beliefs. Sometimes he felt overwhelmed and suffocated by the lies and the duplicity of which he had become a central figure. But he preferred to live with this rather than go back to being penniless and destitute. Money had not bought him happiness, but it certainly made his life, especially that of his mother, very comfortable. His real God was money but what it bought with it plagued him like the devil.

Chapter 5: The Gospel business

The use of 'miracles', 'prophesies' and other 'supernatural' performances was a strategy to attract more believers and keep the ones already in the church.

Angel thought that Bishop JJ was justified in saying that if these poor souls did not come to the CHG church, they would either be lost or getting exploited by someone else. But when he was a deacon in the ZCC, Bishop JJ believed in saving souls, he believed a true personal relationship with Jesus Christ transcended any worldly thing. He believed in the words of Jesus as in Luke 10:7: 'Eat and drink at their table; for the labourer deserves his wages'. He served the members of the church without expecting anything in return. All that had changed was that Bishop JJ had adopted a different philosophy to Christianity. He now believed that for the church to survive and grow its membership, it had to be a business first and church second. He was prepared to do anything in the name of Jesus to raise money. By making people believe he was anointed by God as a prophet, he could call on them to give up their money in the voice and authority of God.

The growing number of members in the CHG church made him a very powerful figure in the country's political environment. His growing influence enabled him to call on favours from politicians and meet any powerful political figures in the country through his local political connections. He secretly donated money from 'his businesses' to politicians on opposing political parties during their election campaigns. He could then call on the favours later when they were in government.

He created a patronage system that filtered all the way down throughout the church. It was built on a hierarchy of favoured people depending on how much money they were willing to seed to 'Jesus Christ', or to be more precise, to Bishop JJ. The more one seeded the more he was connected to the inner circle and got to be seen with the Bishop. They got to be known on a first name basis and got home visits. To get these privileges one had to seed or at least have the capacity to seed really big.

Under the CHG Church doctrine, preached by Bishop JJ, Angel and all their pastors, if one is faithful and obedient to the church they would get material rewards. The more they 'gave to Jesus', or the more 'seeds they planted', the more blessings and riches they would reap.

To display that God was giving them rewards for their seeds, the poor and middle class people who constituted the majority of the Church's membership, outdid each other to show off their designer clothes, latest electronic gadgets and shiny cars.

The church's pastors and their wives led by example in this regard. They came to church in the most expensive cars wearing the most expensive designer clothes. Sometimes Angel struggled to reconcile some of the Bible's teachings and the church's doctrine and practices. The church's philosophy was in direct contrast to Paul's teachings in his letter to Timothy. 1 Timothy 7-10: 'For we brought nothing into the world, and we can take nothing out of it. But if we have food and clothing, we will be content with that. Those who want to get rich fall into temptation and a trap and into many foolish and harmful desires that plunge people into ruin and destruction. For the love of money is a root of all kinds of evil. Some people, eager for money, have wandered from the faith and pierced themselves with many grief'. As far as Angel was concerned, Paul basically confirmed that their church was heretic and dangerous to its followers. But the money was good.

The CHG church enterprise was now a very successful and growing business. Money was coming from all directions to the church through member's donations and ticket sales for various events. More money came from sales of videos and pictures of the 'prophets walking on water' and performing other 'miracles'. These were sold to both church members and anyone willing to buy them. The 'walking on water' videos sold like hot cakes as it was a 'miracle' rarely performed. Church members who paid a tenth of their salary to the church without fail for at least 12 months got free videos. The water from the tub of baptism was also to be put into smaller 500ml bottles and sold as 'holy water'.

Bishop JJ was impressed by Angel's money making ideas. Videos, books and pamphlets of the sermons were also a great source of revenue. The church was now involved in a diversified array of business ventures, from property investments, farming, foreign currency exchange and the share market.

One of Bishop JJ's favourite and highly successful money making schemes was to get trusted fundraisers to sit in strategic areas within the congregation during a service. As his sermon reached its highest point, Bishop JJ would demonstrate how God can instantly reward people with riches. He would then ask the followers if anyone of them wanted to receive God's money rewards right away. Almost everyone within the congregation would raise their hands. One person was 'randomly' selected by the Bishop to come forward and stand next to him. He then asked the rest of the congregation to show their gratitude to God by coming forward and blessing this chosen sister or brother with any amount of money they might have. People would come forward and throw whatever amount of money they had at the chosen person's feet. Church ushers then collected the overflowing money into a box on 'behalf' of the blessed individual.

The first movers to come forward were the Bishop's trusted fundraisers with fake donations. This trick encouraged other followers to genuinely donate money to this blessed individual. Meanwhile, Bishop JJ would be preaching words of encouragement in the background and the church choir sang songs that praised those who had the courage to 'thank God' by giving to this 'poor soul'. At the end of the service, the so called 'poor soul' got a small percentage of the real donations. Bishop JJ's small clique of trusted fundraisers were always keen to volunteer for this scheme as they got rewarded for participating.

By the time Angel left South Africa to start a new church in Zimbabwe he estimated the CHG Church and Bishop JJ were worthy over a hundred million rands in cash and assets. It was hard to tell which assets where Bishop JJ's personal ones and which belonged to the church. No one except the Bishop and the church accountants really knew how much the organisation was really worthy. There was only one signatory to the church's accounts, Bishop JJ himself.

Despite all that was happening in his life, the rising to becoming a 'prophet' and becoming the second most senior person in the CHG Church. Angel never forgot two things. One, to visit his brother in prison and two, to send money and look after his mother in Zimbabwe. He always communicated with her to let her know how he and Don were doing and to find out what was happening back home. On this occasion, he called her to let her know that Don was about to be released from prison. His mother was happy to hear the news and was hoping Don would be able to visit and come and see his now grown up child.

His mother had sad news for Angel. She told him that John, the young man who travelled to South Africa with Angel had just been buried in Zimbabwe.

Angel had last seen John in Mafikeng nine years ago and had never been in touch with him. Apparently John had become a successful entrepreneur. He had started by selling electronic gadgets at the bus station while working at the hotel. He progressed to owning a number of tuck shops around Mafikeng. His businesses had diversified into taxis that transported people and goods between South Africa and the southern part of Zimbabwe. He had also become a big donor to the Mafikeng branch of the African National Congress. His business acumen and political connections had brought him a lot of wealth as well as a lot of enemies. Although he had a well-fortified house and a security guard, one night robbers came to the house, they killed the security guard and shot John in the head. He died at the scene. Nothing was taken from the house, raising suspicion that he was either killed by jealous business rivals or political opponents either from the opposition or from within the ANC. He was given a big funeral in Bulawayo with well-known ANC political figures and businessmen attending.

It had been five years since Angel was evicted from Hillbrow and Don was due to be released from his incarceration. Angel had timed his departure to coincide with his brother's release.

A week before he was to leave South Africa for his full time posting to Zimbabwe, he made his last visit to Johannesburg prison to pick up his brother. Don was to stay at Angel's house with him and Anna, who was now eight months pregnant, prior to the whole family moving to Zimbabwe at a later stage.

A day before he was due to fly out of South Africa to his next destiny in life, Angel put five thousand rands into a back pack and with two bodyguards he drove to the shanty town of Alexandra. As they slowly drove around the pot holes, they passed where his two friends were burnt alive. It seemed like a very long time since the horror he had experienced in this place. New shacks had been built and there was no evidence of any fire ever taking place.

Not much had changed, the poverty was still everywhere. The stench of rotting rubbish and raw sewage seemed worse than he could remember. They meandered around the dusty roads towards the tuck shops. The person Angel was looking for, old man Sam, was still sitting in the same spot where he left him four years ago. He was still basking in the scorching sun.

They parked near the tuck shops and Angel got out of the car. Old man Sam thought they were some high profile ANC visitors. But then he thought, it wasn't election time, so what would they be doing here. Maybe they were looking for someone and had just stopped to ask for directions, he thought.

When Angel greeted him by name, for a few seconds he wondered where this smartly dressed man knew him from. Then his mind connected the voice to the face and he immediately changed from surprise to happiness. He hugged Angel so tight; he was grateful to see that he was still alive.

After chatting to him for a few minutes, Angel gave Sam the backpack and said in Xhosa, "Thank you, may God give you happiness for the rest of your life." Before attracting too much attention from the few people who were around the tuck shops, Angel quickly got back in the car and they drove away. He left the shanty town for the last time a very happy person.

Six months after getting married, nine years after arriving in Hillbrow with nothing and four years after running for his life from Alexandra, Angel landed in Harare. He arrived to a hero's welcome from an already sizable following. The CHG Church had done some ground work in marketing his name as the greatest 'prophet' the country would ever see.

In South Africa, he was known as a native South African born in Zimbabwe. This narrative was very common for most of the Zimbabwean nationals who were in South Africa illegally, particularly those from the south of Zimbabwe who shared similar surnames with a lot of South Africans. In Zimbabwe, Angel was known as the home boy who went to train as a minister, pastor and 'prophet' in South Africa. He was now back home to continue the work that he was called to do. In any case, his followers did not care about the cover story of his origins, as far as they were concerned, he was a man of God. They couldn't care less if he came from South Africa, Zimbabwe or the moon.

Angel's arrival into the country's word of faith business was perfect timing. The chaotic political atmosphere in the late 2000s had resulted in an economy on a downward spiral. A significant number of companies were shutting down, relocating or going out of business. Workers were being laid off left right and centre, and for those who still had jobs, the uncertainty was enough for them to worry about their job security. People were prepared to work for months and months without pay, just to keep their jobs. The result was that the vast majority of the population was suffering. Inflation was skyrocketing and the Zimbabwe dollar was going the opposite direction even quicker. Food was scarce and expensive. There were long queues for virtually any basic commodities all across the country.

In the charged political atmosphere, people blamed the government and wanted it out, the government responded with violent repression. Skilled personnel needed to build the country's economy were voting with their feet in large numbers. Criminal activity, corruption and prostitution were increasing. The gap between the super-rich and the extremely poor was getting wider and wider. The exodus of economic refugees was separating families and resulting in ever increasing numbers of divorced couples. The country was going through the most negative metamorphosis since independence.

The ordinary men in the street could neither afford to leave the country nor had the skills required to legally migrate. It was a very difficult time and a time to turn to God. Gospel music was topping the charts like never before and every musician was clamoring to come up with a gospel track. New churches were popping up on every corner. There were no barriers to forming new churches, it was probably the most successful business next to criminality.

It was evident to the CHG Church that this was a ready, lucrative and perfect market. There was an abundance of takers of their prosperity gospel doctrine in a large population seeking divine solutions to their mounting problems. The increasing number of poor people bought into the doctrine that offered a hope for survival. For the dwindling middle class it offered hope to gain the riches that only a few politically connected individuals were apparently flaunting.

Angel did not waste time to capitalise on this opportunity. He set out to spread the word of faith that promised fulfillment of dreams, divine inspired material riches and endless hope. In the process he was to make more money than any other prosperity gospel business in Zimbabwe.

He promised those joining the church and making large donations, especially the monthly tethers, a potential to live a life of fullness and well-being. He promised them healthy lives and financial freedom. He promised them an un-chaining out of the desperation of unfulfilled dreams and dashed hopes by traditional churches and other prosperity gospel churches. He used the tactics that had worked so well in South Africa, performing magic tricks and calling them 'miracles'. The appearance of 'miracle money', 'walking on water' and prophesying big events, propelled 'Prophet' Angel, the CHG church and their spiritual father, Bishop JJ, to the front pages of leading newspapers, TV screens and radio shows.

The more they were visible, the faster the membership grew and the fatter their bank accounts got. In the first nine months, the church grew from just a few hundred followers to more than ten thousand. One-fifth of the church members had already pledged ten percent of their monthly salaries. Even Bishop JJ was astounded by the way the church in Zimbabwe was growing under 'Prophet' Angel's leadership. Ever since he left the ZCC, he had never seen the church grow at this rate. Money was now flowing back to South Africa as opposed to the first couple of months when they were still establishing their presence. It had been more than a worthwhile investment.

'Prophet' Angel became a larger-than-life figure who was attracting the attention of politicians from all political divides. Political leaders were falling over each other to be seen with him as this might be construed as an endorsement of their ideas. Angel had learnt how to deal with this situation from his spiritual father, Bishop JJ. He would be seen with any politician who was seeking his attention but would sell their meetings as a gospel and spiritual guidance meeting. As a return, the church would later call on special favours from these politicians, particularly those from the ruling party.

The intelligence community was another very important connection the church was going out of its way to attract. Nothing attracted the intelligence operative more than money. The church needed the right connections and the right amount of money to be able to buy the much needed and crucial information for its 'prophesies'. The influence of the church over a large following was sometimes viewed with fear and skepticism by some governing politicians, especially if the church members were suspected of supporting the opposing party. So the CHG church needed the intelligence connections to find out which politicians were not happy with the church's activities and why. Their strategy, again borrowed from their experience in South Africa, was to secretly increase support for the politician in question, like making charity donations to the poorest in their constituency and inviting them to come and present the goods. This way they could kill two birds with one stone. They would get on the good or neutral side of the politician and they would also be able to publicise the church's charitable activities in the hope of attracting more membership.

Political and intelligence organisation connections were also used to silence the most vocal critics of the church through intimidation, denying them a voice in the state controlled media or paying them to shut up.

'Prophet' Angel conducted most of his sermons in English with a bit of Shona which he had learnt growing up in Bulawayo. His childhood friends, like Joel, who belonged to the apostolic faith sect, also known as Mapostori, spoke Shona, and Angel picked it up from them. Angel had also polished his Shona language skills while still in South Africa by taking lessons before he came to Zimbabwe.

Chapter 6: The past comes knocking

Three years had passed since he came back to the land of his birth and 'Prophet' Angel was at the top of his game. He had more money than he had ever dreamt of. He had a beautiful wife, a son, Abel, and a daughter, Angela. His word was law within the church in Zimbabwe. He had access to anyone who mattered in the country, politicians, judges and ministers in the government. He had a security team led by his brother who doubled up as his henchmen. He had followers who trembled and knelt down at his sight and believed his every word. Instead of preaching the word of the gospel, his word *was* gospel. Some of his followers believed that touching him would bring unprecedented good fortune and prosperity. He called people who opposed him all sorts of names and threatened them in front of his ten to fifteen thousand weekly congregations and still his loyal followers saw him as a man of God.

One week he would preach forgiveness and the next, vengeance on the church's enemies, and still his devoted followers failed to see the deception. His influence amongst the public was the envy of every politician. His newly found power was intoxicating and made him feel invincible and untouchable. He was now convinced that he was a true 'prophet' of God. He believed that he was above humans and was not answerable to any of them. He had been given the power to give and take life on God's behalf. There were many testimonies of women who said they managed to have babies after the 'prophet' had prayed for them. And other testimonies came from relatives of dead people who testified that their relative died because they had refused to believe that 'Prophet' Angel was a true prophet. It was not uncommon to hear him say he was God during his many sermons. From a distance, his spiritual father, Bishop JJ, watched this with concern, even he or anyone he knew had never pushed the envelope this far. Because the money was rolling in, Bishop JJ had no intention of putting the brakes on his golden goose and he doubted that he could, even if he wanted to. Spreading his church to Zimbabwe had been so successful that he was already grooming two other 'prophets', one for a CHG church in Zambia and another in Mozambique.

At the same time, Angel was secretly assisting a former methodist pastor in starting his own independent church in Zambia. Pastor Martin Musonda came to settle in Zimbabwe from Zambia in the early 80s. He was assigned to run a Methodist church deep in the rural areas of Mashonaland East. He was stationed about thirty kilometres from Goromonzi. In 2008, he met 'Prophet' Angel in Goromonzi and admired the way he was running his church. He also longed to go back to Zambia as the economic situation in Zimbabwe was now at a point his family could not bear. They became good friends and 'Prophet' Angel agreed to help him leave the Methodist church and go back to Zambia to start his own.

With 'Prophet' Angel's financial and logistical support, within a year Pastor Martin was running one of the fastest growing churches in Zambia, based in Lusaka. His experience as a Methodist minister and support from 'Prophet' Angel made it easy for him to start and grow the church in a short space of time. The church had no connection to the CHG church and Bishop JJ had no knowledge of its relationship to 'Prophet' Angel. As far as he was concerned it was one of the growing competitors to his expansion plans into Zambia

The lavish lifestyle of those in the inner circle of the Zimbabwe branch of the CHG Church, particularly the 'prophet' and his family, knew no bounds. Bishop JJ insisted on the Zimbabwe church investing twenty percent of the member's tithing, collections and proceeds from sales in Angel's name or names of companies he controlled, and eighty percent in Bishop JJ's name or names of companies he controlled. The investments were made in a diverse number of businesses in and outside the country. The majority of the money was invested in South Africa, the United Kingdom and the United States. An investment team for the Zimbabwe branch had been formed as soon as the money started rolling in. The team reported directly to 'Prophet' Angel although they knew Bishop JJ was the man at the top. Their lavish lifestyles were strictly funded from the returns of these investments.

Some of the church's projects were also funded from these returns. This way, Angel would be defended from accusations that he was using the church's money to fund his lavish lifestyle. The church's public relations team would argue that on the contrary, the 'prophet of God' used his own personal money to fund the church. Personal money that he got from his vast business empire across the world. This kind of explanation, although still riddled with unexplained holes of how he came about his vast business empire, was enough to convince the already converted followers.

Bishop JJ had taught 'Prophet' Angel over the years, while he was still in South Africa, that the church would neither win nor would it want to win the hearts of those who criticised the lifestyle of its 'prophets'. So these defense tactics were never meant for those who were outside the household of faith, but were meant for the believers, and therefore they did not have to totally make sense. Besides, believers would never equate their small individual contributions to the massive amount of money needed to fund the prophet's lavish living standard. They would never imagine that each small weekly or monthly contribution from tens of thousands of members added up to millions of dollars annually to the prophet's personal investments.

All this money, power and self-actualisation left Angel feeling like he was still missing something. This was until one day someone came knocking on his door. His brother Don told him one morning during their breakfast that the security team had informed him that a mentally disturbed man had been coming to the gate for the past three days wanting to see the 'magician' and each time he had been turned away. The guards told the man there was no magician who lived in the 'prophet's' house. This was strange to the security guards because they had heard the 'prophet' being called all sorts of names, like pastor, priest and father, but never magician.

The first two days they turned him away thinking he was a mental patient. On the third day they had reported the matter to the heard of security, Don. Don informed 'Prophet' Angel that they expected the man to turn up again that day, which was a Thursday. Don had decided to let 'Prophet' Angel know about this man, as he remembered that 'Prophet' Angel used to be a magician in his previous life. 'Prophet' Angel felt a sense of trepidation but asked Don to let the man in if he came back and let him know as soon as possible.

At midday, like clockwork, the man turned up at the gate and asked to see the magician. To his surprise, the guards let him in. To them this was not unusual as the 'prophet' prayed for a lot of mentally ill people. The visitor was taken to a reception area and given a drink and some expensive looking biscuits by a model-like housemaid. He could not believe the opulence of this place.

While he was still mesmerised he heard a voice come from behind him. It was a voice he had not heard for a very long time, "Hello Karlos."

He stood up and was face to face with his old friend and secret lover, Angel. "Hi Angel," Karlos responded as the two long time partners hugged.

'Prophet' Angel felt that missing bit of his life fulfilled with Karlos in his arms. The realisation that someone could walk in while they hugged brought the two men back to reality. They let go of each other and sat down.

"It's good to see you after such a long time," said Angel as he sank down into the soft cushion of the couch opposite Karlos.

"It's good to see you too. I heard you had made it big," said Karlos looking around the room. "But I didn't imagine you had made it this big."

"Have you been following my life in the church since my days at Diepsloot?" asked Angel rhetorically. "Yes, I am a man of God now and He has given me lots of blessings as a reward."

"Yes, I've been following your progress from a distance, but after Blair died I ..."

"Blair is dead?" Angel interjected in surprise.

"Yes, Angel, he died. He was ill for almost a year from prostate cancer and he died six months ago."

"So what have you been doing since then?"

"It's been a tough time my friend, Blair's relatives chased me away from his funeral and then a month ago they evicted me from our house."

"So where have you been living since then?" asked a concerned Angel.

"The first person I thought about was you soon after Blair died. I could not go back to my family, they disowned me a long time ago, besides I have not been in touch with any one of them for over ten years. Life is difficult enough as a straight man with no job in South Africa, as a gay man it's even more difficult," said Karlos with tears in his eyes. "Blair left me some money, but that has almost run out as I have been moving from place to place living within the gay communities since I was evicted."

"So how did you find me?" asked Angel, curiously.

"I had a lot of help from your old friend, the pastor at your old church in Diepsloot. See, I thought the best place to start when I was looking for you was to go and talk to him since you had done a lot of work for them. So I went to see him and told him I needed to get in touch with you."

"And he gave you this address, just like that?" asked Angel in disbelief.

"No, no, no, I told him about you and me —"

"You did what?" 'Prophet' Angel interrupted in a raised voice, leaning forward from his couch.

"You've got it wrong, Angel, I didn't mean it like that. I mean I told him you were a childhood friend and I needed to contact you about very important family matters. At first he did not want to tell me anything. But after gaining his trust by spending time and money at the church and helping out every weekend, he started opening up. He told me about how you rose quickly within the church to become the star pastor."

"What else did he tell you?" asked Angel with interest.

"After parting with five thousand rands and buying him a lot of beer, he told me everything, some things I did not believe. Look, the man is bitter and jealous that he is still in Diepsloot and you are living here," said Karlos, stretching his arms to point to the luxury around him. "He told me you were making millions. He also said stuff about your wife that I found hard to believe."

"What about my wife?" asked Angel.

"That your wife's first child Able —"

"You mean Abel," Angel corrected him.

"Yes, Abel," Karlos said in agreement. "Apparently Abel is not your biological child, and your wife was a prostitute who came to the church for redemption, already pregnant."

Angel felt a rising wave of anger building up in him, quickly turning into fear with sweat running down his spine. He was getting a bad feeling about how much Karlos knew about him and the reason why he had come to see him.

"He also told me stuff about your second child, Angel."

"My second child? Angela?" asked Angel, stunned but curious to hear more.

"Yes, Angela. He said she is not your biological child either, but your brother's child. He said it is an open secret within the church amongst the pastors that you haven't had sex with your wife since you left South Africa."

Angel could not believe what he was hearing. These were things that he thought only him, his wife and his brother knew about. He leaned forward even further to listen more carefully as he could see in Karlos's eyes that he was not done yet. Before Karlos could continue Angel asked. "Who else have you told all this to?" Immediately he regretted asking that question. He had just displayed his vulnerability.

"No one, I couldn't do that to you Angel. Can't you see? All this gave me hope that you and I could pick up from where we left off now that Blair is gone."

"Just slow down a bit Karlos; what is it that you want from me?" Angel asked, confused. He was thinking all along that Karlos was going to use all this information to blackmail him.

"I need a life, Angel, money and a place to live but most of all I need you back in my life."

Angel could not take this anymore, Karlos did not just want bits and pieces, he wanted everything. He felt Karlos knew too much to be rejected offhand otherwise he could do something irrational with the information he had and completely ruin him. If what Karlos knew got to the media or any of his many critics it could be disastrous, not only for his family, but the entire CHG church in Zimbabwe. He needed to buy some time to think of a way out of this.

"Look, I think we can make this work," Angel said in a calm whispering voice. "I just need a couple of days to come up with a plan of how we can be together while I continue with my work for God without raising suspicion. In the meantime, I will give you some money and get you a place of your own. But for the next couple of days to a week you have to stay in a hotel while I organise everything."

"I do not want to live in a hotel forever," said Karlos as he realised Angel was prepared to do anything for him. Although he was not sure if this was because he still loved him or he was too scared of him because of what he knew. In his heart, he wanted so much to believe it was the former. In any case, he felt good at the prospect of having a place he could call home again.

Angel introduced Karlos to his family as an old friend from his days in Alexandra. Karlos stayed at Angel's house for the rest of that day, and later in the evening Don drove him to a five star hotel in the city where he was booked in to stay for five days.

That night was the longest night Angel had ever experienced since his days in the South African slums. He felt his sense of invisibility slipping away. The missing piece that he had longed for had now turned into a nightmare. The prospect of picking up where he and Karlos had left off was bringing a guilty warmth inside him, but the prospect of losing all the money, power and influence frightened him even more. All of a sudden his life seemed to be at a crossroads and all available roads where dangerously attractive. He felt attracted to all of them but was terrified by the consequences of each.

As the light of dawn started to filter into his bedroom, he had made up his mind that the fantasy of going back to Karlos would remain that, a fantasy. One way or another he had to get rid of Karlos before his secrets were revealed. He thought about paying him off, but realised that he would always be back for more or may not even accept the offer. Trying to reason with him to go quietly and build his own life away from him was tempting, but Karlos had come a long way with deadly information and was not likely to accept that route. He had told him all that information in an effort to make him realise that if he did not comply with his wishes, he was going to tell anyone prepared to listen. There were plenty of people and media outlets prepared to listen. Even his proficient public relations team would find it hard to fight this one. Karlos had to go and go soon and for good.

Chapter 7: Un-prophesied murder

After breakfast the next morning, 'Prophet' Angel requested to talk to his brother privately in the garden. The two men took a walk out into the beautiful rose garden, immaculately maintained by the two garden workers.

Before Angel could say what was on his mind. Don asked, "You seemed to know that gay South African guy very well, is he someone from your past?"

"How did you know he was gay?" asked Angel.

"He told me."

This answer surprised Angel as he wondered what else Karlos had said.

"Yes he is someone from the past, and I want him to stay in the past before he destroys me and the church."

"Do you want us to make him disappear?" asked Don, realising how anxious his brother was.

"Make it clean and make it quick," said Angel as the two men reached the centre of the garden adjacent to the swimming pool where one of the garden workers was clearing leaves out of the water.

The 'prophet' had spoken, his word was gospel and Karlos was now a dead man walking.

By that afternoon Don had hatched a plan. He called the South African cell phone number of his former cell mate at Johannesburg prison, Bigboy Modise. They had spent three years together until Don was released.

Bigboy was released eighteen months after his cell mate left prison. He was popularly known as BM for big mouth. Bigboy never stopped bragging about having killed all kinds of people from little kids to a ninety-year-old woman. Originally from Venda land he had told anyone who was prepared to listen how he escaped prison. He was serving a life sentence after being arrested for killing his pregnant girlfriend and dumping the body into the Limpopo River to be eaten by crocodiles. Few people believed his many seemingly exaggerated stories of killing people, but Don knew him well enough to know he would do anything for the right amount of money. BM was always available to hire at the right price.

That same afternoon in Johannesburg, after talking to Don, BM hired a black seven series BMW sedan. He was going to drive to Harare that evening, getting to the address Don had given him the following morning. It was going to be an easy two day job for a cool fifty thousand rands. It was a great opportunity he could not pass up. He was familiar with the route to Harare as he had travelled there on several smuggling missions.

As agreed with Don, he would carry five thousand rands for expenses like toll gates and police bribes, both on the South African and Zimbabwean sides of the border. He was a bit worried about the Zimbabwean side of the border, particularly on his way back. The deteriorating economic situation had made it easy for him to bribe his way through any checkpoint. But there were now too many of these checkpoints both official and fake. It was going to take him ten hours to get to the said address, he would then rest for most of the day and drive back to South Africa late in the afternoon.

Meanwhile in Harare, soon after talking to BM, Don called the hotel where Karlos was staying to let him know that a house was ready for him to move into. He was to check out of the hotel the following morning and Don would come and pick him up to take him to the house.

Karlos fully trusted Angel but could not bring himself to like, let alone trust, Don. The excitement of having a place to stay that he could call home again overrode his mistrust for Don. He believed that the message came from Angel and he understood the reasons why Angel would not talk to him directly. After all, he was not the same struggling magician he knew from Alexandra. He was now the leader of the biggest prosperity gospel church in Zimbabwe. He could not go anywhere without being mobbed by both fans and media. He could not speak to anyone or be seen with anyone without people asking questions. Karlos would have to be content with seeing him discreetly as and whenever he was available.

At exactly ten o'clock the following morning, Don arrived at the hotel in the company of a mean looking big man with a knife-like scar across his chin. Don introduced him as Andy, the church's deputy head of security.

While Karlos and Andy packed Karlos's bags into the tinted window Toyota Prado parked at the hotel car park, Don made his way into the hotel lobby to make a quick phone call and pay Karlos's hotel bill.

They left the hotel and drove around the city's central business district, stopping at various shops where Andy bought groceries and clothes. Every time they left to buy stuff, Karlos was told to stay behind in the car.

When they left the CBD they drove along a two lane highway for about an hour, ending up in a high density suburb that resembled a South African township. All along the conversation between the two men, although conducted in Shona, which Karlos could hardly understand, showed that they were more than just employee and employer. Karlos suspected they must have also been very good friends. At the township, they stopped at one house where they dropped off the clothes. Two young kids came running out of the house, calling Andy daddy. Karlos assumed this was Andy's official residency. Andy went inside the house for about ten minutes while Don played outside the house with the kids who were calling him Uncle Don.

They left the house and drove around the township for another twenty minutes before stopping at another house. While the two gentlemen offloaded the groceries from the car, a woman carrying a small baby walked out of the house and kissed Andy, handing him the baby. She greeted Don and did not seem to notice that Karlos was in the car. She picked up the groceries and disappeared into the house. While Andy played with the baby, Don helped take the remaining groceries into the house. From the way the lady behaved, Karlos assumed that she was Andy's second wife. After another half an hour at the house they continued their journey.

They drove through the township for another half an hour before entering the highway and drove at relatively high speeds for an hour and half before entering what looked like a low density suburb. All along the two gentlemen continued to talk, joke and laugh, completely ignoring Karlos. The street names in this suburb where all in English as opposed to the ones he had seen in the township which were mostly Shona, with one or two in English.

It was just before three in the afternoon when they stopped outside an address which stuck in Karlos's mind because of its familiarity. It was number 23 Alexandra Street. The address of the house he had lived in with Blair was also number 23 Pitt Street, Alexandra West.

As soon as the car stopped outside the gates, the two metre high gate automatically slid open, revealing a big colonial style house. They drove into the driveway towards a double garage which was part of the house, passing two saluting security guards in black uniforms. To the right side of the double garage, partly obscured by the neatly trimmed trees, was parked a black seven series BMW with South African number plates. The Prado drove into the garage and the garage doors automatically closed behind it as it stopped.

"This is where you will be staying my friend," said Don. "There is a guest here at the moment, but he is leaving tonight, after that you will have the whole house to yourself," he continued while opening the door to get out of the car.

Karlos felt relieved and relaxed but very hungry. Now that they had finally made it to their destination he could settle down and hopefully find something to eat. He got out of the car's back passenger seat from the right side to make his way to the boot and retrieve his bags. At the same time, Andy, who had been driving all along, was getting out of the driver's seat. He walked behind Karlos to the back of the car. Karlos assumed he was coming to help him carry his bags. As he bent to pick up his bags from the boot, which Don had just opened, he felt a hard knock on the back of his head, he lost consciousness and collapsed on the garage floor.

Earlier that morning, BM had arrived at number 23 Alexandra Street just after nine. Driving mostly at night, he had met only two traffic check points on the South African side and one on the Zimbabwean side of the border.

The security guards at the house were expecting him and let him into the house. He had parked his car off the driveway next to the garage. The yard was well kept, the lawns well-trimmed and the flowers were so well pruned and looked after only a professional gardener could have done it.

The house was empty but with signs that it was regularly used. The kitchen was loaded with all sorts of different types of foods both in the refrigerator and in the cupboards. BM walked around the house which had four bedrooms and a single big bathroom with a shower and a bathtub. Three bedrooms were locked except the master bedroom whose door had been left open.

After taking a shower and having breakfast, he made himself comfortable on the large couch in the living room to sleep. At 10am the phone rang as he was just drifting off. It was Don confirming that BM had arrived at the house. He quickly fell asleep after the phone conversation.

He was startled out of his sleep by voices coming from the bathroom. He checked his wrist watch: 3.20pm. He felt refreshed and ready for the long drive back to South Africa.

While still unconscious on the garage floor, Andy and Don tied Karlos's feet together and his hands behind his back using rope they found in the garage. Then they carried his lifeless body into the house and onto the bathroom floor. Don turned on the taps to fill the bathtub.

When the water was half way from filling the tub, Karlos started regaining consciousness; his head felt as if it weighed a ton, he could hear water running as if from a distance. He tried to open his eyes and move his arms, but his body wouldn't move. Even his voice wouldn't come out of his mouth. Just then he could make out two figures entering the room and could hear voices. The water stopped running. Andy and Don then lifted him up and put him in the bathtub face up. The cold water seemed to bring him back to life and he opened his eyes and realised that Don was staring straight at him. Don could see the terror and surprise in Karlos's eyes.

Before he could say anything Don spoke. "You will never be able to bother the prophet again," he said with a deadly sounding voice.

Before Karlos could say anything, his head was pushed down into the water. He tried to struggle, wiggle and kick, but his whole body was held down and the two men were too strong for him. He struggled for what seemed like eternity but it was hopeless. Eventually, his body went limp and lifeless.

"I think he's done," said Andy as he let go of Karlos's legs.

"Bring the body bag and lets lift him out of the tub," said Don as he let go of Karlos's head. "We have to wake-up Bigboy so he can move his car into the garage."

The two men quickly lifted Karlos out of the bathtub and put him into the body bag.

"You can go and wake him up and I'll go and open the garage door. Make sure he reverses his car into the garage to make it easy to load the body," said Andy as he dried his hands leaving the bathroom.

Don walked into the living room and greeted his former cell mate. BM returned the greeting, moving his feet down to the floor and sitting on the couch still half asleep. Don did not sit down, he just tossed the towel he was using to dry his hands on the floor. He then went into one of the locked bedrooms and came back with a black briefcase.

He handed it to BM and sat down saying, "There is thirty grand in there as agreed, five for your expenses and the remaining twenty-five you'll get in Johannesburg when the job is complete."

"Thanks," said BM as he opened the briefcase to see the contents. He quickly closed it without counting the money.

"You have to start moving now so that you can get to the river before it gets too dark," said Don.

"You're right," replied BM as he stood up to leave.

"Reverse your car into the garage and we'll load the goods."

"Ok," said BM, smiling at the thought of the money in the briefcase, his mind already on what he was going to do with it.

After BM parked his car in the garage next to the Prado, Don and Andy put Karlos's body into the boot of the BMW and closed it. Just after 4 pm, the security guards at the gate saluted as BM drove out of number 23 Alexandra Street.

Within an hour he had left the city and was speeding down the highway towards the border. Two hours after he left the house, as the sun was beginning to set, he passed a small town half way between Harare and Beitbridge. In another two hours he should be crossing the border into South Africa he thought.

Angel was sitting in his study finalising the preparations of the next day's sermon when the phone rang. Before picking it up he checked his wrist watch, it was 6.05pm. It was his brother on the phone. He told him that Karlos had been taken care of and wasn't going to be a problem anymore.

After putting the phone down, he felt a cloud of depression, guilt, emptiness and cognitive dissonance descend on him. He now wished he had never given the order to get rid of Karlos. He wished he had tried harder to find a better solution to deal with the issue. He could not hold back the tears that ran down his cheeks. He did not realise how much he still loved Karlos, his death now felt more like a loss than a relief.

Mr. Modise felt the road getting rougher and rougher. He thought slowing down a bit would make it better, but it did not. The steering wheel was getting heavier and required a bit more power to keep the car under control. The car was pulling to the right towards the middle of the road. He passed a sign showing that there was a lay by a kilometre ahead. He thought it would be a good opportunity to take a break and have a look at the car.

At the lay by, he pulled off the road and got out of the car and immediately realised he had a flat front tyre. It was getting dark, so the sooner he could change the tyre the better. He quickly opened the boot of the car, rolled Karlos's body further inside the boot and got the jack and the spare wheel out. He closed the boot and was soon lifting the car to remove the flat tyre.

He was about to loosen the last of the five wheel nuts when he saw car lights brighten the space he was working on, a passing car slowed down and stopped. It was a small army jeep going in the opposite direction. Two soldiers got out to come and help him.

They had helped a lot of stranded strangers along this road many times as they always travelled up and down this route. It was getting dark and the man changing the tyre was in a dangerous part of the bush which was well known for highway robbers. Within moments the soldiers had helped remove the flat tyre and put on the good one. One of them removed the jack while the other took the flat tyre to the boot. BM was tightening the last wheel studs thanking the two gentlemen for their assistance when he heard a loud scream from the back of the car.

"Oh, shit! There's something moving inside your bag," shouted the soldier who had taken the flat tyre to the boot. He stared at the wiggling bag under the car boot light.

"What? Are you a poacher?" asked the other soldier.

"No, no, no," said BM, trying to find the right words to justify what the soldiers had just discovered.

Before he could say anything else the soldier at the car boot had put the flat tyre down and was opening the bag.

"It's a man!" he shouted

Immediately the soldier standing next to BM grabbed him and dragged him to the back of the car. The soldier who had found Karlos quickly untied him and lifted him out of the car boot. He was only half conscious and could hardly move his body or say anything.

"He's still alive, we have to take him to hospital," he said as he carried Karlos on his shoulder to their jeep.

"And you're coming with us," said the other soldier as he took the ropes that had been used to tie Karlos and used them to tie BM's hands behind his back.

He frog marched him to the jeep and sat him in the back passenger seat. The soldier helping Karlos had put him on to the front passenger seat and was now seated at the driver's seat ready to go. The soldier who was dealing with BM ran back to the BMW and locked it. He jumped back into the already moving jeep and they sped away in the direction where BM had come from.

BM was too stunned at the quick turn of events. How could it be possible that this man was still alive? He felt angry at Don's incompetence. He was only an hour away from his destination, and the money! Then he remembered, the money had been left in the car. This was his chance to get out of this predicament.

"Wait, I have thirty thousand rands in the car, you can have it and let me go, please. It wasn't me who wanted this man dead. Please, I will tell you everything," begged BM.

The soldiers were very skeptical about what he was saying. They thought he would say anything to get out of the situation. When BM kept insisting that there was money in the car, the driver thought to himself, if this is true this is more than three times their annual salary. He stopped the jeep and turned around to face BM and said, "If you're lying about the money, you will be in worse trouble than you are already in, do you understand?"

"Seriously, I'm not lying," begged BM.

"We might as well turn back and take this man to Beitbridge hospital, it will be better than clinics at the Growth Point, which might be closed at this time of the night anyway," said the second soldier who was sitting next to BM.

Within minutes the jeep was parked next to the BMW and the soldier who had been driving was searching for the briefcase that BM had described. It did not take him long to find it under the front passenger seat. He opened it and could hardly believe his eyes when he saw bundles of brand new R100 bank notes packed tight and full inside the briefcase. He quickly snatched a bundle, put it in his pocket and closed the briefcase. He locked the BMW and was soon back in the Jeep.

"Let's go, I got the money," he said.

"So he wasn't lying?" asked the other soldier, smiling at the prospects of keeping the newly found money. "What are you involved in man? Are you some kind of a hit man or drug dealer?" the soldier continued.

"No, I never touched this man, I was only paid to dump his body into the Limpopo River as close as possible to where the crocodiles live. Now that you have the money, please, let me go, I'm begging you," pleaded BM.

The jeep sped south towards Beitbridge hospital. BM kept on with his pleas for mercy but to no avail. In less than an hour after leaving the spot where they picked up BM, the soldiers arrived at the hospital.

They took Karlos inside, who was still barely conscious, leaving BM in the car. His hands and feet were tied up so he couldn't run away.

After giving all the relevant information to the
doctor and nurses, they left the hospital for the police
station. They handed BM over to the police, who took
their statement and locked BM in the cells. Nothing
about the money they found was mentioned in the
statement. By midnight, the soldiers passed the spot
where all the drama had begun, they were on their way
to the capital city R30 thousand richer. It was the last
time BM ever saw them or his money.

Chapter 8: The Crumbling

Angel picked up the Sunday morning newspapers and browsed at the headlines as he always did on his way home from church every Sunday. He used the remote control to lower the radio volume.

All the headlines carried the same story, another bus accident the previous night involving cross border traders on the way to Beitbridge. This time nine people had died. It was the third accident in a week involving buses from the same company. Different newspapers gave different reasons for the cause of the accident. Reasons ranged from bad roads to a drunken driver, who unfortunately was one of the deceased. One newspaper quoted a former employee who said the buses from the company where not road worthy because the company put profit first and passengers' and the driver's safety second. He said drivers were forced to work very long hours and it was common for them to fall asleep at the wheel.

The one that caught Angel's attention was the newspaper that mentioned witchcraft as the cause. He picked it up to read further. The paper was quoting another former employee who was now working as a manager for a rival bus service on the same route. He claimed that the bus owner planted people in all these buses that had been involved in accidents who immediately harvested dead people's body parts after every accident. These parts would then be sold for witchcraft purposes and also be used to strengthen the bus owner's businesses. He also claimed that all these bus accidents happened at night to provide cover of darkness for the body parts harvesters. During the night, help is not likely to come to the scene quickly.

Angel went further into the newspaper to read the editorial comment. The editor's comments did not mention the witchcraft idea but pointed to the two decades of economic decay and infrastructure decadence as the root cause of the high number of fatalities and road accidents. High unemployment was driving people to embark on these dangerous journeys in buses that where basically death traps. Unrepaired roads, shortages of genuine spare parts for the vehicles had all come together to produce the unacceptable number of road fatalities. The editor called on the withdrawal of transportation licenses for all bus companies that were found to be operating passenger vehicles that weren't road worthy. He suggested that this was not likely to happen because most of the business people operating these killing machines where politically connected.

Just below the editorial comment another small story caught Angel's attention for a moment. It's head line read "South African man arrested with body in the boot". During his days in South Africa, this kind of news would never have made it to any part of any newspaper. It happened almost every day. He put away the newspaper as the car drove into his driveway.

Meanwhile, that same morning, Beitbridge hospital had seen a hive of activity since the early hours. They were treating many seriously injured bus accident victims. It was now besieged by reporters from all local newspapers chasing more news on the bus accident story.

There was one reporter who was interested in pursuing the story he had started the previous night. His police source had not given him much except that the victim was still in hospital and the police would interview him as soon as he regained consciousness. He wanted to get to the victim first before he spoke to the police and before other reporters picked up on the story. His hospital source had just told him the victim was making very good progress and was expected to be talking by the next day.

What was more sensational was that the man arrested for the crime was claiming to have been hired by 'Prophet' Angel's brother. He was also claiming that 'Prophet' Angel was directly involvement and that he had 30 thousand rands when he was arrested. But police considered his claims as rantings of a delusional mental case. Besides, they were reluctant to point a finger at the politically connected 'prophet' or anyone related to him for fear of losing their jobs. But the reporter was not going to let the story die.

Early the next morning, which was Monday, the reporter was taken into Karlos's room by his hospital contact. He was told he had twenty minutes as the hospital administrators would be starting work soon and the police would be coming soon after. Karlos was still confused and not sure who to trust. The reporter introduced himself and told him briefly what he already knew and wanted him to fill in the details.

Karlos started his story from the time he met Angel up to the time he mastered all his swimming skills to hold his breath under water while Angel's brother was trying to drown him. He had been unconscious from then on, but remembers dreaming about two soldiers coming to his rescue. He told the reporter how he tracked down Angel through a pastor at Diepsloot and what the pastor had told him about Angel.

The reporter could hardly keep up with making notes. He had come expecting just a small confirmation but he had actually stumbled upon the story of his career. This was one of the most intriguing stories he had ever come across. Ever since the rise of the prosperity gospel and it's many rich prophets in Zimbabwe, he had been one of their biggest critics. Now he had proof that the prince of the prosperity gospel doctrine and one of its most adored stars was not only a fake but was gay too.

As he left the hospital through the back door, he saw the police car drive into the car park. That evening, before sending his story back to his editor, he double-checked his story with his police source. Karlos had virtually told the police the exact same story he had told the reporter. Police had charged the South African man with attempted murder and kidnapping. They had also obtained a warrant to arrest Don, 'Prophet' Angel's brother, and Andy, the deputy head of security of the CHG Church in Zimbabwe. By the end of that day a message had been sent to the police in Harare to find them.

'Prophet' Angel was woken up just after 6.30am on Tuesday by a phone call from his brother who was in a heightened state of panic. He told him that the headline story in the Bulawayo Daily Post was saying that there was a warrant out to arrest him and Andy. He told him that the newspaper claimed that Karlos was still alive. He was at Beitbridge hospital and was talking to the police. He also told 'Prophet' Angel that the man he had hired to get rid of Karlos's body had been arrested and had mentioned Don's name to the police. The more Angel listened, the worse the news got. The devastating news was that Karlos had told a reporter everything. Don said he needed money to get out of the country as soon as possible. For a moment, Angel thought it was all a dream and he was still sleeping. Then he remembered the small headline in one of the Sunday newspapers and realised that it was from the same newspaper Don had just mentioned.

He felt physically sick. He felt a tremendous wave of fear, his whole body was very cold, his heart started to beat rapidly, he could hardly breathe and he felt dizzy. He tried to think of a solution quickly. He held onto the phone in silence for what seemed like an eternity. When he came to his senses, he asked Don to get a car and drive towards the Mozambique border via Nyamapanda. It would be the quickest route out of the country and the least likely to have police check points. He would meet him just outside the city and give him enough money to find his way to South Africa. The idea of going down south sounded like a good idea to Don as it was a familiar place. He had plenty of places to hide there. Places him and his friends had used before during his days as a robber.

At exactly 11am that morning 'Prophet' Angel met his brother on the side of the road just outside the city. He gave him 100 thousand rands to make his escape and find a place to stay in South Africa until things cooled down.

At the same time, a team of plain clothes detectives where putting handcuffs on Andy at his residence in the township. Another team was raiding the house at 23 Alexandra Street. They were looking for Don and any evidence that would help them in their case.

As he drove back into the city, 'Prophet' Angel thought about the unfolding events. If Karlos was talking and his brother somehow got arrested, it was a matter of time before they came for him and that was just the criminal side of things. He had seen the Daily Post headlines Don was talking about. They read: "The prophet's brother wanted for attempted murder". There was nothing about his relationship with Karlos yet. But he knew sooner or later it was going to come out. The court of public opinion was already in session. Even the church's public relations team would have a hard time fighting this one.

His thoughts turned to what Bishop JJ would say about the sudden turn of events. When he got home he called the Bishop to let him know what was happening. Bishop JJ told him to come back to South Africa for a while, starting the following week. He was to leave after the next Sunday service. Bishop JJ was sending the pastor he was grooming for the mission in Zambia to come and take over in the interim. During the coming week, 'Prophet' Angel was to try and deal with the public relations fallout and let the church lawyers deal with the legal side of things.

'Prophet' Angel did not tell Bishop JJ that he had ordered Karlos to be terminated and had helped his brother to run from the authorities. After talking to JJ he asked Anna to pack and leave the following morning. She had to take as much cash as she could carry, take the kids and leave them with 'Prophet' Angel's mother in Bulawayo. Then she would have to travel to the CHG headquarters in Jabulani in South Africa. Angel would meet her there early the following week. He told Anna that he was looking for Don and did not know where he was.

The different newspaper headlines of the following day reflected the growing deteriorating situation around 'Prophet' Angel and the church. According to the newspapers, Andy had confirmed to the police that Don and him had tried to kill Karlos. He had also revealed other dirty laundry about the church, including that a number of high ranking male church members, like him, had mistresses looked after and supported by church resources. He had also confirmed Karlos's story that the Prophet did not have any biological children as commonly known. And that the church had a vast empire of businesses both in and outside the country. There was only one person who controlled the empire's funds and that it was the 'Prophet' himself. He claimed that the whole church system was based on patronage, no one dared say anything negative about the 'Prophet' or oppose him. Anyone who did would be cut off from the church's direct support or from doing any business with any other entity directly or indirectly controlled by the church or its members.

By Thursday, the headlines began to link 'Prophet' Angel to the attempted murder. That whole week's news read like a soap opera. People could hardly wait for the next day's news to see if Don had been found and what he had to say. People were filled with anticipation for any other surprising twists the story would take.

The Bulawayo Daily was the top selling newspaper that week. The publication was printing twice its normal runs and was selling every copy. To divert attention, Angel asked the church's public relations team to buy a whole page advert in all daily papers from Thursday to Sunday to advertise a special sermon on Sunday. It was to say God has heard the people's cries and prayers and was to reward them with 'miracle money' at this special service, which would be held on Sunday at the end of that week. The service would be called The Deliverance Day and would be free of charge.

After saying goodbye to his brother, Don left the city boundary and sped north east. He had never been on this road before. But he figured if he stayed on the main road for about four hours, he would be at the border crossing by late afternoon. He was relieved that he did not meet any police check points, just villagers waiting at bus stops that he passed along the way.

The border crossing seemed deserted in the hot late afternoon. As he came closer, a policeman carrying an AK 47 rifle appeared from the shade nearby and asked him to leave his car unlocked and go inside to get his passport stamped. The passport officer took his passport and stamped it, but did not give it back to him. He asked him to sit on the bench just next to the counter while he waited for the policeman to confirm that there was nothing in the car to be declared. He had been sitting for about five minutes when the policeman came into the room still carrying the gun but also carrying the briefcase with R100 thousand Angel had given him. He was quickly detained in a holding cell while the border authorities determined where he got the money from. They also wanted to know why he was travelling to Mozambique with such a large sum of money via this particular border post. He further raised the suspicion of the two officers when he tried to buy his way out by offering them some of the money to let him go.

It wasn't until two days later, on Wednesday morning, when another customs officer came to relieve his colleague that they discovered who Don was. The officer brought with him the old newspapers of the last couple of days, Don's face was on the front page of one of them with the words "WANTED" written under it.

A phone call was placed to the police in Harare and by Friday night Don was back in the city, detained at the central police station cells. Just as had happened to his former cell mate, BM, Don never saw or heard about the R100 thousand that was taken from him at the border post.

Memories of his time in Johannesburg prison came flooding back. He could hardly stand the cells in Johannesburg prison, but they looked like a hotel room compared to the filthy cell he now found himself in. As he sat on the hard cold concrete, he looked at the old tattered blanket covering what looked like cardboard paper on the iron bed, he wondered how long he would live in such a desperate situation. He prayed that his brother would be more successful in fleeing so that he would not have to endure what he was facing. He vowed that he would rather die than sell his brother out like BM and Andy had done.

'Prophet' Angel realised the game was up when he read the Saturday morning headlines, "Prophet's brother finally found" said one newspaper. "Prophet's brother arrested trying to flee" said another. "Murder case. Net closes in on the 'Prophet' as brother is arrested" said the one that had already linked Angel to the attempted murder case.

He spent most of the day preparing the following day's sermon with the assistance of the new pastor Bishop JJ had sent.

Unknown to 'Prophet' Angel, Bishop JJ had instructed the new pastor to take over the church as he now considered 'Prophet' Angel an unredeemable liability. He was afraid 'Prophet' Angel's scandals would destroy the CHG church in Zimbabwe. The new pastor was to take the lead in the following day's sermon and any other ones to follow. Before going to bed that night 'Prophet' Angel called his mother to talk to the kids and to tell her that he loved her. He told her that he was sorry for everything, for the wrongs he had done to her and all the people who followed his church. To Angel's mother, it felt like the last goodbye to her favourite and most successful child, she could not help but shed a tear.

On Sunday, the church was packed full. It had been built to accommodate twenty-five thousand people, but today there must have been over thirty thousand. Another five thousand or so were outside, unable to enter the packed building.

There were the regular attendees plus the lapsed members who had come for the promised 'miracle money'. There were those curious to hear what the prophet might say about the events of the last week and reporters hoping to catch a scoop. 'Prophet' Angel introduced the new pastor, who stood up and gave the opening prayer and introduced the theme of the sermon then sat down. 'Prophet' Angel took to the podium to do the main preaching. The theme of the service was, taking personal responsibility after deliverance.

"Let us start by reading Luke chapter 16:10-12 'He that is faithful in that which is least is faithful also in much, and he that is unjust in the least is unjust also in much. If therefore ye have not been faithful in the unrighteous wealth, who will commit to your trust in true riches? And if ye have not been faithful in that which is another man's, who shall give you that which is your own?'"

You have heard people say, take care of the cents and the dollars will take care of themselves, I say take care of the small blessings or opportunities God has given you and the big opportunities will be many. Stop crying about your job not paying you enough, save the little that you get from that small job and invest to earn more. Stop giving that little you have to other people by buying things on loan or taking loans that charge you high interest. That is not being responsible with the little blessing God has given you. Stop envying and trying to live like your next door neighbour, who by the way is most likely being irresponsible himself trying to stay better than you.

"Let's read further, in chapter 16:13 Luke goes on to say 'No servant can serve two masters, for either he will hate the one and love the other or else he will to one and despise the other'

"By the same token, if you are earning very little, you cannot be responsible and invest your hard earned money and live like a rich man at the same time. You cannot live a high life on borrowed money and invest for your family's future at the same time. The result of living beyond your means on borrowed money is more debt, spending all your hours labouring at work just to pay your creditor. By the way, your creditors are very intelligent people who have seen an opportunity to make more out of their hard earned money by giving it to you, the unintelligent person. Remember what Solomon said in Proverbs 22:7 'The rich rule over the poor, and the borrower is the slave of the lender'. Do you want to be a slave all your life? Wake up and take responsibility for your own small, but God given opportunities so that God can entrust you with bigger opportunities tomorrow. Stop putting value in things that do not add any value to your life. Before you spend the fruits of your labour on anything, ask yourself whether you need it or you want it. If you just want it, forget it. Only spend on necessities and invest the rest.

"Let's listen again to what Jesus says about using our opportunities in Luke chapter 19:12-28: 'One day a rich lord was going on a long trip. He wanted his servants to take care of his property while he was gone, so he called them to him. To the first servant he gave five talents of money. The man went to work at once using his master's money until he had doubled it. The master gave the second man two talents of money. The second man was successful too, and doubled his master's money. To the third man the master gave him one talent with the expectation that he would also manage it well, but he dug a hole and hid it in the ground. And after a long time the rich lord returned to come and reckon with his servants. The man who had received five talents brought his money and showed the master that he had doubled it. The master was well pleased. He said, "Well done good and faithful servant you have been faithful in a few things, I will put you in charge of many." The man that had been given two talents showed the master that he had also doubled his money. The master was well pleased. He said, "Well done good and faithful servant, you have been faithful in a few things so I will put you in charge of many." The man who had received one talent of money went and dug up the talent he had buried and brought it to his master. He gave it back to him and said "here is what belongs to you, I feared you because I knew you are a harsh man who reaps where you did not sow." The master was very angry with him and called him a wicked and lazy servant. He said the least the man should have done was to put the money in the bank and received interest. So the master took away the one talent he had given him and gave it to the man who had produced ten talents. The wicked and lazy servant was punished because he had not properly used the little opportunity he had been given'

"Although this parable's teaching has lessons that go way beyond financial responsibility and investing. It clearly shows that God does not like people who when given opportunities, big or small, either do nothing about them like the wicked and lazy servant or waste them, ending up with debts they can barely pay. God wants you to be rich like the first two good servants; he does not want you to be stupid and poor like the wicked and lazy servant. Some Christians shy away from speaking about making money and getting return on investment as if it's a sin. Here Jesus tells us that our God rewards those who utilise the opportunities they have been given and punishes those that waste them.

"I have been talking a lot about investing your savings. Some may ask how they can do that. The Bible has given us the basics; it even has examples of great investors in the old holy book. Let us read about King Solomon's advice on investing in the book of Ecclesiastes 11:2: 'Divide your portion into seven or even eight, for you do not know what misfortune may occur on earth'. In other words, King Solomon is telling us to split our small savings into several investments and not to put all our eggs in one basket.

"Investment diversification is one of the most important fundamentals of wealth creation. King Solomon gives us another very important investment lesson in the book of proverbs 24:3: 'By wisdom a house is built and by understanding it is established.' That is, do not put your money in investments that you do not understand. Remember if an investment is too good to be true, it most likely is. You will not be able to build a solid and growing portfolio from complicated businesses that you have little or no knowledge of.

"Last, but not least, the company you keep will determine your investment returns. If you associate with losers you will be a loser, if you associate with winners, like members of this great church, you will be a winner. If you keep the company of good investors you will learn good things about investing.

"   Let's hear what King Solomon says about this in Proverbs 13:20-21: 'Whoever walks with the wise becomes wise, but the companion of fools will suffer harm. Trouble pursues the sinner, but the righteous are rewarded with good things.' Remember my friends, do not make money for the sake of getting richer than your neighbour, but do it only for the sake of doing good for the Lord.

"As I leave you today, my friends and relatives in Christ. I would like you to remember the words of my most admired writers, Orson Welles. Words that always bring me down to earth and remind me that there is more to life than making money and getting rich. 'We're born alone, we live alone and we will die alone. Only through our love and friendship can we create the illusion, just for the moment, that we're not alone.'

"Make the most of this moment my friends, I pray, that you make the most the of it, because before you know it, it's all over, Do not waste your time being judgmental and prejudiced against anyone, based on their race, tribe, colour, religion, gender or sexuality.

Prejudice is the child of ignorance. Be quick to forgive, remember we are all human and that means we are all sinners. Remember to thank God every day before going to bed for the day he has given you; thank Him every morning for keeping you safe while you slept and giving you the next day. Use that day wisely for there is no guarantee you will make it through to its end. There isn't enough time in your life to be doing valueless things like holding grudges, regrets and repeating your mistakes. For anger consumes the angry and not who they are angry with, regrets do not change your circumstances and those who do not learn from their mistakes are bound to repeat them."

As he finished saying these words while the crowd was silently contemplating what he had just said, 'Prophet' Angel lifted his hands to the sky. Then said "God rewards these people with the blessing that you promised them for the seeds they have planted." A pop sound followed coming from the direction 'Prophet' Angel's hands were pointing. When the crowd looked up, they saw R10 rand notes raining from the Church's ceiling. Immediately there was pandemonium. Everyone forgot about 'Prophet' Angel and was trying to catch as many notes as they could. The notes were everywhere, and people where falling over the furniture and crashing into each other to catch the falling 'miracle'. It was like a riot had just broken out. The church stewards tried in vain to control the crowd.

Word quickly spread to the crowd outside that money was raining inside the church. They tried to get inside, while others were trying to get out, blocking the entrance.

When it was all over, eleven people had died, including two children, and scores of others had been injured. Ambulances and riot police were on the scene to pick up the injured and to control the crowds respectively. There was blood on the floor, and shoes, bags and other personal belongings were scattered everywhere.

'Prophet' Angel sneaked out of the church without anyone noticing as soon as the stampede for the raining money started. He got into his car and drove back home as quickly as he could. As he turned in to the street towards his house he wondered about the irony of the current situation. When he was sitting at the back of the car being driven around, he was driving events in his life. Now that he was driving himself, events seemed to be driving his life.

No one was at home besides the security guard stationed at the gate. He was surprised to see the 'Prophet' driving himself as he always had a driver with him. 'Prophet' Angel went through the automatic garage door and closed it behind him. He hurriedly got into the house, picked up the two suitcases that he had packed and locked the previous night. One had his clothes and another was packed full of American dollars. He put the suitcases in the car, opened the garage and drove out. He looked at his wrist watch, it was 5.20pm. Again, the security guard was surprised to see his boss leave twenty minutes later, but just waved him goodbye as he drove out of the gate.

He was the last person reported to have seen 'Prophet' Angel 'alive'.

The following day at six in the morning he stopped at the Hwange service station. He was disguised in a cap and dark glasses and was wearing a cheap track suit. After paying for the fuel, he picked up the morning paper as he made his way to his car. His picture was on the front page with headlines reading, "11 people dead as miracle money rains at CHG church. 'Prophet' Angel disappears". The only other story on the front page was about an earthquake in Haiti killing 230,000 and destroying the majority of the capital Port-au-Prince. It was all about death, he thought, then threw the paper out of the window. He looked left and right before pulling on to the main road. Taking off his dark glasses he mumbled to himself "Life is certain, death in certain, everything in between is just a theatrical illusion" as he sped north west towards the Zambian boarder.

The police and the media frantically looked for Angel for months without any success. On several occasions rumours would circulate that he was seen in a certain town, and police and journalists would descend on the town only to come up empty.

Three months after he disappeared, his car was found parked in the bushes deep in the Victoria Falls National Park. It was still locked with everything intact but without all the four wheels. Police could not find any fingerprints in or outside the car, it had been wiped clean. His passport had never been registered at any border crossing as having left the country.

After spending a year looking for him without success, the police gave up the search and assumed he was dead. There were numerous speculations about what might have happened to him. His most adherent followers believed that he was taken to heaven on the day of the raining 'miracle' money. Some even testified that they saw his body being lifted up into the sky as the money came down. Another theory was that he made his way back to South Africa to a secret place were his wife was waiting for him with hired assassins. They killed him, took all the money he had and got rid of his body. Some South African newspapers suggested that he came back to the CHG church headquarters where Bishop JJ, seeing him as a liability to the whole church, got his henchman to eliminate him. Some said he went overseas, possibly Britain or America, where he started a new low profile life within the gay community. And others believed he drowned or was eaten by crocodiles trying to cross the Zambezi River into Zambia. Despite all the conspiracy theories, Engelbert had vanished into thin air.

Chapter 9: John Lungu Resurrected.

My name is John Lungu formerly known as 'Prophet' Engelbert Ncube. I have been reborn with my true identity. John Lungu was the name and surname that I should have had when I was born had it not been for the extraordinary circumstances at the time of my birth and the discrimination my father experienced because of where he came from. It has been six months since I crossed the crocodile infested Zambezi River from Zimbabwe into Zambia, hiding in a fisherman's small canoe. I considered this a fourth defining moment in my extraordinary life. The first was when I was born dead with the name John and rose with the name Engelbert. The second was when I left Zimbabwe via Botswana looking forward to a new life in Johannesburg. I had so much hope and expectations of a much better life than the one of poverty and deprivation I had grown up in. But that turned out to be a nightmare which climaxed when I found myself running for my life out of the shanty town of Alexandra. Those terrifying moments marked the third critical juncture in my life and turned me into a very successful and wealthy preacher. The crossing of the Zambezi River that Sunday morning and tossing my passport over board became the fourth crossroad in my life and I am not sure if this will turn into another nightmare or if it is the start of another success story.

But I am determined to make it the latter. I ran from the authorities in Zimbabwe because in a moment of panic I asked my brother to get rid of someone. It was a bad idea that turned into a tragedy.

I preached the scriptures according to my own interpretations and I lived the scriptures on my own terms. In Luke 16:9, in the parable of the shrewd manager, Jesus says "And I tell you, make friends for yourselves by means of unrighteous wealth, so that when it fails they may receive you into the eternal dwellings". I made a lot of these friends with the money we conned from members of the Christ's Happiness Gospel Church and Pastor Martin Musonda was one them.

I have been hiding here in the Zambian town of Choma in one of Pastor Martin's safe houses for the last six months. He is based in Lusaka where his church's headquarters are based. I have a new Malawian identity complete with an identity card, passport and driver's license, thanks to him. I am slowly changing my looks by gaining weight, keeping a beard and much longer hair than I used to have. I am also taking this time to think about my next step.

When Pastor Martin heard the news about my brother's disappearance before he was arrested, he called me to find out if he could help. Up to that time I had only one choice, that is, to do what Bishop JJ had instructed. I was to go back to the base in Soweto. I did not trust our Bishop. Eventually he would have traded me in to the authorities in exchange for the continued survival of the CHG church in Zimbabwe. He was the kind of man who could sell his own mother to keep his golden goose, the CHG church. If he thought I was a liability he could have got his henchmen to get rid of me. Besides, I was suffocating in that life and I needed to completely cut it loose. Pastor Martin's offer to help seemed to be God sent. He arranged for fishermen to pick me up in the Victoria Falls National Park and bring me to a homestead in rural Zambia, near the border with Zimbabwe. I left my car in the bushes of the national park after cleaning it of any traces of my fingerprints and locked it. I then threw the keys into the mighty Zambezi River together with my Zimbabwean passport.

Pastor Martin had been in this rural part of Zambia many times to see his wife's parents. He was very familiar with the smuggling routes used by the local people to buy food in Zimbabwe in the early 80s when the Zambian economy was on its knees. Back then, basic commodities were in very short supply and very expensive. I stayed in the rural homestead as a guest of his youngest brother-in-law for a week while Pastor

Martin got me my new identity. His wife's parents had since passed on.

One person I was really worried about day and night was my mother. Her eldest son had vanished in South Africa, another son was now in prison. And me, I was now presumed dead after they found what was left of my passport in the Zambezi River. Well, technically, the man known as Engelbert Ncube was 'dead'. I was trying hard to think of the best way I could send my mother a message telling her I was still alive and well, without alerting anyone else.

After six months of much contemplation I was getting bored with reading the Bible and watching TV most of the time. I was getting very lonely as there was hardly anyone in the house besides the occasional cleaner and the gardener. I had also gained almost twenty-two kilograms above my normal weight. So I decided it was time for me to say thanks to Pastor Martin for his hospitality and start doing something with my life. He arranged a driver to pick me up and take me to the airport in Lusaka.

It was on a Tuesday morning the first week of August when I said goodbye to my dear friend Pastor Martin at Lusaka airport. I boarded a plane bound for Johannesburg. It was refreshing to get back to the city of gold as a new person. Somehow, somewhere within my heart, I was feeling relieved to have left Engelbert in the Zambezi River. I had become a prisoner of my success.

I stayed in a suburban motel for a while before renting a small flat in Kempton Park. My aim was to go to Kimberly and find my brother or at least find out what happened to him, then try and find the best way of relaying the information to my mother. This was the least I could do for her after what we had put her through. Besides, I always felt guilty that I should have done this for her while I was in South Africa before I left in 2006. She was almost sixty years old now and she was not in the best of health. Raising all those grandchildren had taken a toll on her. Strangely, of all my siblings, I was the one who had given her the most help and yet none of her many grandchildren where my biological children. The fact that I was the last born and her favourite child compelled me to do whatever it took to help her. I was her Angie, the name she used when I was a child. I never used to like the nickname when I was young. I remember every time she shouted my name while I was playing in the dusty streets with other kids, I would immediately shout back a response and run straight home. She probably thought I was a good boy, but I only did so as to stop her from shouting that name a second time. It suddenly occurred to me that she was the only person who called me by that horrible nickname. If I sent her a message and said it came from Angie, she was most likely the only person who would know where it had come from.

Once I had settled in my new place, I decided to go to Kimberley. As I drove south west past Klerksdorp in my rented Toyota pick-up truck, I started to wonder where I would start from. I had never been to Kimberley. It had been about eighteen years or so since Themba went to Kimberley. This was really a long shot. I wasn't even sure if he continued using this name after coming to South Africa as some Zimbabweans changed their names to ones that sounded more South African.

After driving for six hours, I stopped outside a motel in Kimberley. It was late afternoon and I was exhausted. I would have to start my quest the next morning.

The following morning I started my enquiries at the motel dining room during breakfast. I asked the motel manager where I could locate retired mine migrant workers. She did not have much information, but told me that most of the retirees in Kimberley would most likely have worked at one of the diamond mines. I was hoping to find at least one from Zimbabwe, particularly from Bulawayo. She gave me a name and address of a shebeen called MaMoyo's in the township of Homevale. She told me to look for older men, buy them a lot of beer and they would start singing about their good old days at the mines.

I left the motel and drove around the townships of Galeshewe, Retswelele and Homestead, just to familiarise myself with the place before going to the address I had been given in Homevale.

I got there just before 6pm. There were two young men outside the house sitting on some comfortable looking chairs under a tent. I asked them where I could find MaMoyo. They pointed me to the entrance of the main house. I knew that people got suspicious of strangers at shebeens. I had to introduce myself to the shebeen queen to make it easy for me to be accepted. She looked younger than I expected, but she was a very pleasant host.

Inside the house were even more comfortable couches arranged around a big round coffee table. There were about 14 sitting places and a giant TV was hanging at the centre of one side of the wall. On each corner of the giant room were some mean looking speakers. I could not see the sound system, but assumed that it would be controlled from another room.

After introducing myself to MaMoyo, I told her about my mission. I told her that I was hoping to find retired miners who might point me in the right direction in tracking my brother. My chubby looks and my protruding belly made me look like a businessman who was about to spend a lot of money. She invited me to the kitchen and served me a delicious traditional meal. There were two other ladies in the kitchen helping out with the cooking and a young well-built man playing with the sound system. I assumed he was the DJ and also kept unruly clients under check. While I ate, MaMoyo told me about the three diamond mines that had since closed down. Some of the retrenched miners had since been hired to work in the refinery that was opened a few years after the mines closed. After the closure of the mines a lot of migrant workers did not have much to show for their years of hard work, so they either never bothered to go back home or could not afford to. They just integrated into the communities, most of them already had families here in Kimberley.

MaMoyo herself was the daughter of a Zimbabwean migrant miner who had since passed on. Because her father died in a mine accident, they had got compensation from the company which they used to buy the house. Since her mother had no other income, she decided to start up a business. The business was named after her mother, not her. The younger MaMoyo had taken over when her mother became ill. The front of the house, which had the kitchen, the sitting room, a storage area and the tent outside, were used for the business. The back of the house had three bedrooms and a kitchen, a sitting and dining room was where the family lived.

After I had cleaned my plate, which was the best value for money meal I had ever had, I would have licked the plate if she wasn't looking, MaMoyo took me to the back of the house to meet her ailing mother and her young son. I felt good talking to MaMoyo's mother, it was like talking to my own mother.

We went back to the lounge where people were beginning to gather. MaMoyo introduced me to one of the ex-miners, who immediately asked for a beer before he would happily give all the information I wanted. I paid MaMoyo for a beer and a soft drink. The miner was surprised that I didn't drink alcohol, but I sensed he was not too concerned as he was too excited and eager to tell his story.

As MaMoyo brought the drinks, another ex-miner walked into the room and was called to our corner by the first. After the introductions, I asked MaMoyo to bring another drink for the gentleman. We talked for about three hours and I kept buying the drinks, but it was clear these two had never met or did not remember my brother. All along I had been hoping I would hear something, a small hint from them that would give me a clue that at least my brother had been here, that someone had seen and worked with him, but

I was disappointed. I did not recognise any of the names they mentioned as having come from Zimbabwe. Just before midnight, I sneaked out into the kitchen and said goodbye to MaMoyo and left the shebeen. I felt a bit frustrated, maybe I had been too optimistic, but I was not ready to give up yet.

The following three days I drove all around Kimberley townships talking to people at the grocery shops, beer halls, municipal offices and police stations. But I did not get any useful information. For another three days I turned my attention to the suburbs. I went to the nightclubs, sports clubs and I even went to a golf tournament, but still there was no trail.

After a whole week, I was getting disillusioned, maybe my brother never made it to Kimberley. This place had such a large population that my search was like looking for a needle in a haystack. I was also getting tired of motel food and takeaways. I was missing home cooked traditional food, so I thought I would pay another visit to MaMoyo before I headed back to Johannesburg.

I had made up my mind that I needed to go and rethink my quest. I was already toying with the idea of putting a notice in some of Kimberley's widely read newspapers offering a reward for any information. The thought of hiring a private investigator also crossed my mind.

MaMoyo was happy to see me and I was equally happy to see her food. She had been doing her own digging for my brother's trail and had been more successful than I had been. She had spread the word among her customers for any information about an ex-miner called Themba Ncube. One of her customers had given her the name of the former mine pay clerk a Mr. Masuku. She had contacted Masuku and as the pay master he knew almost every waged mine employee. He used to run an illegal money loaning business at the mine, charging exorbitant interest rates. A lot of the miners were his clients. He never had any problems with bad debtors. As the pay clerk, he deducted his loan repayment first before paying his clients. Fortunately, Masuku remembered the Ncube surname and the two close brothers. One of them was his client, but the other one had vowed never to borrow money from him. I couldn't thank MaMoyo enough. After having my dinner I stayed for another couple of hours to chat with some customers and bought more beers. I came back the following morning as per arrangement with MaMoyo to go and pay Masuku a visit.

Mr. Masuku lived in New Park. He had retired when the mine closed. He had used his retirement money and the money from his extortion business to purchase a lot of properties from the mine which he was now renting out. I guessed that was the reason he could afford to live in a relatively expensive house in the suburbs. Yes, he knew the Ncube brothers, but could not remember their first names. I knew Themba had no blood brother in South Africa, so I was still skeptical that I was on the right trail. To avoid disappointment, I told myself maybe Themba had met someone from Zimbabwe who shared his surname and they became good friends. It was very common in most African communities to call someone who shared your surname or came from the same village your brother.

Mr. Masuku remembered that one of the brothers, who was his client, drank a lot and the other never touched alcohol. He also remembered that the one who did not drink used to refer to people who drink and drive as baboons or monkeys with loaded guns. I felt joy in my heart when I heard him say that. Only Themba would have remembered those words from our mother. For the first time I felt confident that my brother had come to Kimberley and I was on the right trail. Mr. Masuku also recalled that one of them was such a good employee that he was recalled by his foreman when the new refinery opened. I could not contain my excitement and eagerness to meet my brother. I kept pressing Masuku to tell us where I could find the Ncube brothers. When he came back to work at the refinery he rented a room in one of his houses in Floors Township for just over a year. Apparently this was near where other brother lived. The other brother wasn't renting any of Masuku's properties so he did not know his address. I was prepared to go door to door in Floors Township if that was what it took to find Themba. Mr. Masuku said he still had access to the closed mine's employee records and he asked me to come back in a couple of days. He needed time to search for the addresses of the Ncube brothers.

I left Masuku's house and went back to Homevale to drop off MaMoyo. As I made my way back to the motel, I felt mixed emotions of anticipation, excitement and apprehension about what I would encounter when I saw my brother after such a long time. I wondered if we would even recognise each other. Maybe we had even crossed paths in the last week and had not recognised each other. I thought about how happy my mother would be to find out that her eldest son was still alive. Before I realised it, I had reached the motel car park.

Two days later I was back at Mr. Masuku's house, this time I was alone. The news I got sent my emotions on a roller coaster. I got the address and first name of my brother's brother. His name was Kabelo Ncube and his last known address was in Floors Township as

Masuku had said. The refinery records listed Themba Ncube as deceased, with the last known address also in Floors Township. I was really disappointed to find out that my brother may have been dead. I did not want to believe it; I needed someone who could collaborate this or even show me where he was buried. I told myself that maybe there had been a mistake on the records. The company records also listed two dependents and a wife as next of kin, but did not have their forwarding address. I had to go and find Mr. Kabelo Ncube without delay. I thanked Mr. Masuku and left.

I arrived at Mr. Kabelo's address mid-morning and the sun was already scorching. An old man was sitting on a bench in the shed under a tree smoking a cigarette. I assumed he must be Kabelo's father or older brother. I greeted him shaking his hand. I told him who I was and I asked if I could see Mr. Kabelo Ncube. Before answering that request, he wanted to know why I wanted to see Mr. Ncube. He move to one side of the bench and beckoned me to sit down next to him, which I promptly did.

I started by telling him where I was from and that I was searching for my brother, Themba Ncube, who I understood had been friends with Mr. Ncube. After listening carefully, he asked me why my surname was different from Themba's. It had slipped my mind that anyone would wonder why I was Mr. Lungu but claiming to be related to Mr. Ncube. I stumbled a bit trying to find an answer that would not bring in my true past. In the end I settled for the familiar story, that I had changed my name when I came to South Africa to one that had a local familiarity. He offered his hand to me for a hand shake, while holding my hand he told me he was Kabelo Ncube and Themba had been his best friend. He was very happy to see me. I didn't like hearing him refer to Themba in the past tense.

He told me that Themba was the best brother any man could ever wish for. Themba had been with him when he went to his in-laws to pay lobola for his wife and was the best man at his wedding. He told me if it was not for Themba he would have died long ago from drinking too much alcohol, or his wife would probably have left him. It was hard to believe that he could be about Themba's age. Alcohol and smoking seemed to have taken a toll on his appearance. I was anxious to know what had happened to my brother, but I sensed that Kabelo was not in a hurry to get to that part. I was prepared to be patient and let him tell his whole story. He narrated their friendship from when Themba came to Kimberley up until the mine was closed.

Themba got married round about the same time he did and had two children, a boy and a girl, just like Kabelo. After the mine closed, Temba took his family and they went to settle at his wife's rural home just outside the town of Prieska. Prieska was about three hours' drive south west of Kimberley. When the refinery was up and running their ex-foreman had come looking for Themba. It was Kabelo who travelled to their rural home to find him. Themba did come and work at the refinery just as Masuku had said, but left his family behind at their rural home. He rented a room not far from Kabelo's house and commuted to their rural home at the end of each month without fail. It was on one of these trips that the bus he was in burst a tyre, overturned and killed ten people, including Themba. I could hear the sadness in Kabelo's voice as he talked about the death of our brother. I wiped off tears that were rolling down my cheeks. It was painful to hear the confirmation of what I had already been told by Mr. Masuku.

He continued, but I was not listening any more. My mind was lost; I was thinking about how my mother would feel to hear that another of her loved ones had died in a road accident. The tears would not stop flowing. I sat there looking down with my hands together and my elbows resting on my knees. I hadn't realised that Kabelo had stood up and was inviting me inside the house to meet his family.

I spent the rest of that day at Kabelo's house and it was now late evening and I was driving back to the motel. I longed to talk to my mother and tell her what I had found out about her son and also to find out what had happened to Don. But I knew I couldn't just pick up the phone and talk to her. So I decided I would continue with my quest as arranged with Kabelo.

It was close to two weeks since I had come to Kimberley. In the early morning, the day after I met him, Kabelo and I were driving south towards Prieka. We got to the town just before ten in the morning. It had been years since Kabelo had been to the rural home where Themba was buried. Prieka town had grown really quickly since then so Kabelo's directions were a bit hazy. After asking around, we managed to find the road that led to the village. The village was only a twenty-five minute drive from the town. It was to the north on the banks of the Orange River.

We arrived at the homestead at about 10:45am. It was a typical rural South African homestead. There were four round mud wall thatched huts built in a circular formation with the doors facing the centere. It was quiet, like there was no one at home. We parked the car near the homestead gate. As we approached the gate, a dog started barking and immediately a lady in her early or mid-forties came out of one of the huts. She squinted her eyes as she tried to make out who the two strangers were. I could see that she had recognised Kabelo by her smile and increased her pace towards him. After greeting each other like long lost relatives that had suddenly found each other, Kabelo introduced us. Her name was Muzi, short for Muziwenkosi. We went into the hut which had a small fire with a small pot on it. The kitchen was the dining and sitting room. We sat on the bench while she sat on the floor. Although there was very little smoke in the hut, I could hardly breathe. My eyes were watering. It took me a while to settle down and get used to the atmosphere. She told us that Themba had rarely talked about his family in Zimbabwe, but he had mentioned that he had two brothers and a sister and that his father had passed on.

We spend the rest of the day talking about our families and eating traditional rural food. She told me about Themba's life and I was pleased that besides the tragic accident, she had mostly happy memories about her life with my brother. I talked mostly about my mother, brother and sister, and their children. I did not say anything about my eventful life.

It was late in the afternoon when the children came back from school. I couldn't be happier to meet them. The girl's name was Sihle and the boy's name was Themba junior. We talked late into the night; I sensed that all this talk about the good times helped Kabelo. He seemed to have never had the time or the opportunity for this kind of therapy. We went to bed with a plan to visit my brother's grave the following morning.

The children did not go to school the following day, so we all went to the grave. The family, or at least Muzi, seemed to visit the grave quite often, as it was well kept.

I put three stones on the grave, one for me, one for my mother and one for Don. I prayed for him to continue his rest in peace. As we were about to leave, I noticed the date of death on the grave, at first I thought my mind was playing games with me. I rubbed my eyes and took a closer look. I stood there staring at the date until Kabelo asked me what was wrong. I told them I could not believe what I was looking at. The date of death on the grave was the same date of death for our sister Sihle. How could this be? It meant that when we were burying our sister in Zimbabwe, our brother was also being buried 2000 kilometres away.

On the way back to the homestead, I thought about how I was going to let my mother know about all of this. It was a mixture of good and bad news. When we got back, I asked Muzi if she would like to take the children to go and see their grandmother. She agreed to do so during the coming school holidays, which were starting in a week and a half. The children were equally happy and excited. They were going to travel outside the country for the first time and also meet their grandmother and cousins. We arranged that they would come and meet me in Johannesburg and I would make all their travel arrangements from there.

We spent the rest of that day visiting Muzi's relatives who were scattered all over the region. Her brother lived with his family in Prieka town. We left the following morning for Kimberley.

I dropped Kabelo off at his house, and gave my heartfelt thanks to him and his wife for helping me find my brother and his family. I promised to come and see them again in the near future.

It was late in the evening when I arrived at MaMoyo's. I needed to thank her and also let her know that my quest had finally been successful. I also could not resist the urge to eat her food for the last time. I left her shebeen at 10:30pm after buying a lot of beers for the two motor mouthed miners I met the first time I had come to MaMoyo's. The following morning, after breakfast, I said goodbye to the motel manager with a big smile.

I spent the following week arranging passports and return flight tickets to Bulawayo for Muzi and her children. I also got myself a one way ticket to Manchester via France. I offered my landlord an offer he could not refuse to purchase the flat I was renting and registered it in the names of my brother's children.

The day before they were due to travel to Zimbabwe, Muzi and her children arrived in Johannesburg. We spent the day shopping for them and for the family in Bulawayo. I let my brother's children buy whatever they wanted, it was the first and last time I would be able to spoil them.

Back at the flat, I gave Muzi a letter for my mother. In it, I told my mother how I had decided to go and find my brother to give her closure about what had happened to him and me. I told her that I hoped seeing my brother's family would give her the satisfaction that he lived a good life and she would be proud of him. I told her I was sorry that I would never be able to see her again, but I was happy, healthy and would try to be a better person in the future. I signed it as Angie. I also gave Muzi the title registration for the flat. I had arranged for it to be rented out with all the furniture in it. She would use the rental money to look after my brother's children.

The following day I took them to the airport and said goodbye to them. I was happy with what I had done, particularly for my mother, but I was still not satisfied that I had done enough for her. I went back to the flat and packed. I looked around the place for the last time before locking up. I dropped the keys at the estate agents and drove to the airport.

After dropping the car at the rental company, I made my way to the international departure lounge. As I went into the door, my heart stopped for a second. Right there at the doorway was my former spiritual father Bishop JJ. He just stood aside, apologised and let me pass. He did not even look at my face. I froze there for a moment, then I went in and he left for his flight. I smiled with joy in my heart. If Bishop JJ could not recognise me, I knew no one would. My next destination: London, United Kingdom, to do what I did best, selling God.

Made in the USA
Monee, IL
07 July 2026